Paper Pandas
and
Jumping Frogs

Paper Pandas

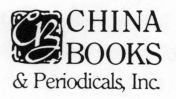
CHINA
BOOKS
& Periodicals, Inc.

and Jumping Frogs

by Florence Temko

Illustrations by Paul Jackson and Florence Temko
Photos by Richard Peterson and David Friend
Book Design by Kathleen McKeown

© 1986 by Florence Temko

Library of Congress Catalog Card Number: 86-70960
ISBN #0-8351-1770-7

First published September 1986.

Printed in the United States of America.

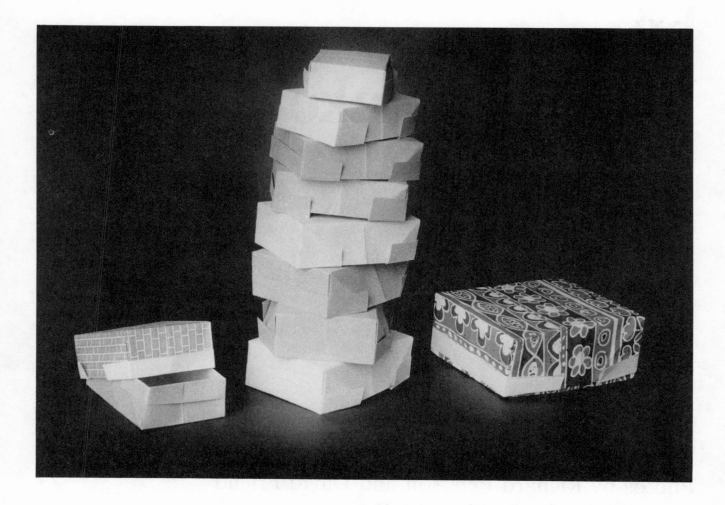

A paper airplane swoops across the room. Just a piece of paper folded quickly, but you may be surprised to know the same piece of paper could be folded into hundreds of other useful things—without any need for cutting or gluing.

Paper Pandas and Jumping Frogs shows you how to make flowers, boxes, puppets, and animals with paper, available from many neighborhood stores. Most projects are designed for beginners, but you will also find a few intermediate and advanced projects, all with instructions tested by people who never folded paper before.

In *Paper Pandas and Jumping Frogs* I have adopted a new approach to an enjoyable craft. I am not only showing how to make paper things, but how to turn them into useful party decorations, giftwrapping, and flower arrangements, and how to use them in other practical ways.

Paperfolding has a long tradition in China. There children learn from parents and grandparents how to make boats, boxes and dollhouse furniture, and paper crafts are also encouraged in elementary schools. In the natural flow of communications, this folk art eventually reached Japan where it developed into the national art known as origami.

In recent years paperfolding has attracted enthusiasts of all ages in many parts of the world, and paperfolding, or origami, clubs now exist in the United States, Europe and Japan. Schools have been particularly receptive to paperfolding as a worthwhile activity that helps students in art, mathematics and social sciences.

Paperfolding is fun, and I will never forget my excitement when a friend first showed me how to make a paper box. But little did I know then that this was the beginning of my lifetime fascination with paper. I hope you will have a good time as you try your hand at paperfolding.

CONTENTS

CONTENTS Cont'd.

ABOUT PAPERFOLDING

The Chinese have a saying: "A journey of a thousand miles begins with a single step." All the colorful paperfolds in this book begin with a single crease and are completed without the use of scissors or glue.

I have written *Paper Pandas and Jumping Frogs* for a general audience of all ages and with a dual purpose in mind:

> To show step-by-step how to fold a piece of paper into animals or objects, and

> How to use the things you fold for everyday and holiday decorations.

When people first become aware of paperfolding they are full of questions. The following are asked most frequently.

Q: I am all thumbs. Do you think I could learn?

A: Sometimes as many as 200 people attend one of my programs and within an hour or less they have all made two or three things, sometimes to their own surprise.

Q: What can you make?

A: Really anything: animals, toys, decorations, magical beasts.

Q: What can you do with these things?

A: Entertain children—and adults, make party and table decorations, greeting cards, mobiles, gift boxes of any size, jewelry, doll house furniture, and shiny Christmas tree ornaments.

Q: How do people get started with paperfolding?

A: Usually they see someone make a bird, a boat or a flower and are sufficiently intrigued to try it themselves. They memorize how to make one or two things with which they may delight others at every opportunity, or they become true enthusiasts wanting to try new paperfolds all the time.

Q: Isn't there a Japanese name?

A: Yes, origami. Ori means folding and gami means paper.

Q: Do you have to use special kinds of paper?

A: Any fairly thin paper, such as notebook, typing or giftwrap paper is suitable. Packages of colorful origami paper of just the right texture, ready cut into squares, are sold in art stores.

Q: Do you always start with a square piece of paper?

A: Most things begin with a square, but a few are made from rectangles, and in rare instances from other geometric shapes.

Q: Isn't paperfolding rather childish?

A: Like any other art or craft, beginners of any age start with simple designs. A finger puppet may be easy enough for a child of kindergarten age, but other figures are so complex they require hours to complete and a lot of experience. Paperfolding has a magic that transcends age.

Q: Is there an underlying technique?

A: Some helpful terms are used by paperfolders, and most of them are quite descriptive and self-explanatory, such as "valley fold," and "mountain fold." A sequence of beginning steps common to many figures is called a "base," for example: kite base, bird base. These procedures are detailed under "Key to the Basics." For existing models, one need only follow directions carefully.

Q: What's a model?

A: Model is a term used to describe the final result.

Q: Do paperfolders invent new patterns?

A: Definitely. Look at paper as an art medium, just like paint or clay, with limitless possibilities for new forms.

Q: How long before I could start inventing my own paperfolding designs?

A: Participants at some of my one-time workshops have come up with new designs, but mostly people begin creating after they know how to make a variety of established patterns and have become familiar with the way paper can be shaped.

Q: Is paperfolding educational?

A: Certainly. It is artistic, stimulates the imagination, helps coordinate mind and hand, and can be used to teach mathematical concepts. Some schools use paperfolding routinely and for class enrichment.

Q: How can I learn advanced paperfolding?

A: From other paperfolders and available books.

Q: I prefer learning from another person. How can I get in touch with a paperfolder?

A: Paperfolding clubs exist in the United States, Japan and many other countries. The following addresses are reliable sources for getting in touch with paperfolders in your vicinity and for supplying other information:

> The Friends of the Origami Center
> c/o American Museum of Natural History
> 15 West 77th Street
> New York, NY 10024 USA
>
> The British Origami Society
> c/o David Brill
> 12 Thorn Road, Bramhall
> Stockport, Cheshire SK7 1 HQ
> Great Britain

International Origami Center
c/o Akira Yoshisawa
P.O. Box #3, Ogikubo
Tokyo 167, Japan

Nippon Origami Association
1096 Domir Gobancho
12 Gobacho, Chiyoda-ku
Tokyo, 102 Japan

Or you can write to me:

Florence Temko
c/o China Books & Periodicals, Inc.
2929 24th Street
San Francisco, CA 94110 USA

The Friends of the Origami Center in New York offers an extensive library on paperfolding, and the Mingei International Museum of World Folk Crafts in La Jolla, California, maintains the Florence Temko Papercraft Collection and Library on paperfolding, papercutting and other papercrafts.

Q: Do clubs have meetings?

A: Yes, and whenever paperfolders meet they get excited over exchanging directions for old and new patterns. They welcome newcomers and share their craft enthusiastically.

Q. Who attends these meetings?

A: People of all ages and occupations: postmen; nurses; elementary, high school and college students; teachers; secretaries; homemakers; dentists; bank tellers; engineers; magicians, the list could go on for ever.

Paperfolding is an inexpensive, portable hobby that can help you establish instant social relationships. Try it!

KEY TO THE BASICS

Crease paper up (Valley fold).

Crease paper backward—away from you (Mountain fold).

Thin line—existing crease made previously.

Arrow points the direction in which paper is to be folded.

Fold paper to make a crease and unfold to the previous position.

Turn paper over, back to front. Top of paper remains as the top.

- - - - - - - - - - -	*Valley fold*
— · — · · — · · — · · —	*Mountain fold*
————————	*Existing crease*
	Direction to fold
	Fold-unfold
	Back to front

Jagged line—Make a Reverse fold, an important procedure to bring a small corner in between the main layers of the paper. Here is how:

Reverse fold

1. Fold the corner in the desired direction. This a helpful preliminary.

3. Let the folded paper open up slightly and push the corner down on the creases already made. (One of the little creases is already a mountain, but the other reverses from a valley into a mountain fold.)

4. Sharpen all creases.

2. Bring corner back to its previous position.

KEY TO THE BASICS Cont'd.

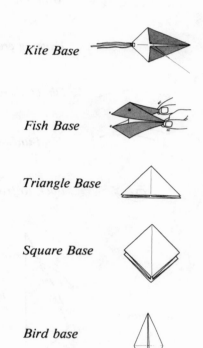

Kite Base

Fish Base

Triangle Base

Square Base

Bird base

Bases

Many things begin with the same sequence of steps, called a "base." The following bases occur in this book.

Kite Base: See Kite drawing 3, page 68.

Fish Base: See completed Talking Whale, page 55.

Triangle Base: also called a Waterbomb base. See Surprise Triangle, drawing 4, page 30.

Square Base: also called a preliminary base, as it is the beginning of the bird base. See The Surprise Square start-off, drawing 4, page 94.

Bird Base: the most versatile of all bases and the beginning of many animals. See Crane, drawing 4, page 97.

How to Make a Square from a Rectangle of Paper

As most projects in this book begin with a square of paper, it is useful to know how to cut a square from paper of another shape.

1. Fold the paper so that the short edge of a rectangle meets the long edge.
2. Cut off area as shown.
3. Here is the square.

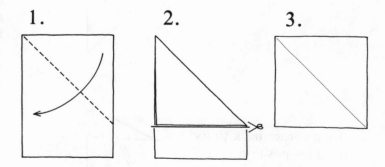

1.   2.   3.

PAPERFOLDING PROJECTS

JUMPING FROG

1.

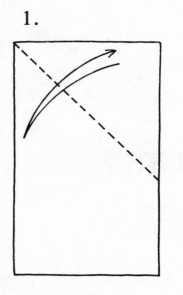

2.

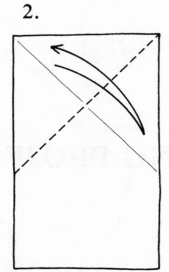

This frog really jumps. Learn how to make it and you can entertain your friends. It's made from a business or index card and if you carry a few cards with you, you'll be ready any time.

Use a business card or a 3"x5" (8x13 cm) index card.

1. Fold the top edge to the long edge. Unfold card flat.
2. Fold the top edge over to the other long edge. Unfold card flat.
3. Fold backward (Mountain Fold) as shown, where the creases cross. Unfold card flat.
4. Push down at 0. Bring up sides X and Y to meet. Then push down and flatten the triangle just formed. See next drawing. Sharpen all creases.
5. Fold the outer corners of the triangle to the top corner.

3.

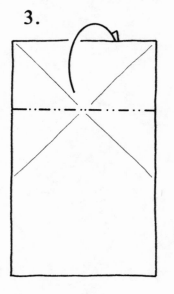

4.

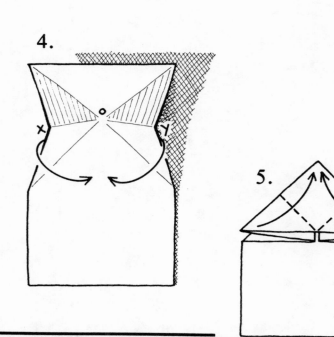

5.

6. Fold the sides of the card to the middle.

7. Fold the bottom edge to the top.

8. Bring the top edge of the front layer to the bottom edge.

9. Loosen the front and back legs a little. Stroke the back of the frog and it will jump.

9.

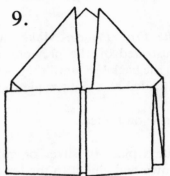

8.

7.

6.

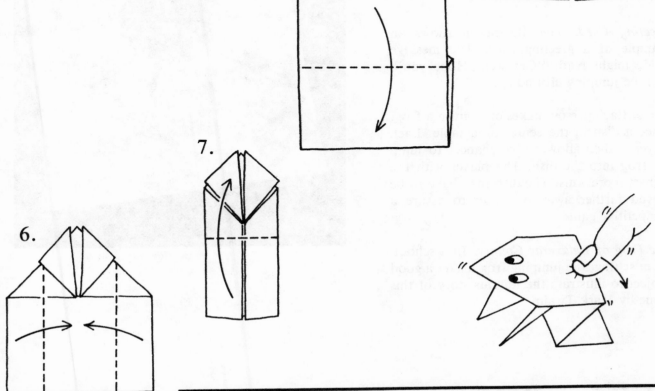

JUMPING FROG Cont'd.

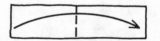  

Options/Uses

The Frog Prince: Make the jumping frog illustrated on the previous page. Straighten up the back legs until they are almost flat and extended at a right angle to the body.

Draw on a face.

Cut a piece of silver or gold paper into a crown and glue it to the head.

Greeting Card: The illustration shows an example of a greeting card. The message inside might read: "Get well. Hope you'll soon be jumping around again."

Game: Each person makes or is given a frog. Place a dish in the center of a table. Each player is then allowed five chances to jump the frog into the dish. The player with the highest score wins. The dish may have to be moved farther away or closer to assure a competitive game.

The Frog of Calaveras County: In a schoolroom setting, the jumping frog makes a good project to illustrate the famous story of this name by Mark Twain.

FINGER PUPPETS

1.

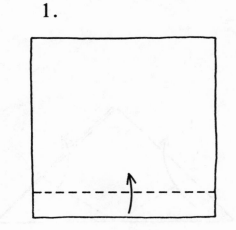

Use a 3'' (8 cm) square.

1. Fold the bottom edge up to form a cuff.
2. Roll paper with cuff on the outside. Slide one side into the cuff on the other side.
3. Draw or paste on paper scraps for facial features.

2.

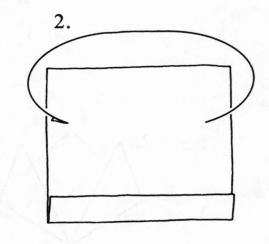

3.

Options/Uses

Characters: Finger puppets can be made into all kinds of characters from fairy tales, comic strips, even outer space sagas. Children will invent their own stories or theatricals, but finger puppets can also be used in the adult world as advertising and marketing tools.

Halloween Creepies: Make longer finger puppets from colored construction paper, and cut the tops into clawlike points.

TULIP STICKER

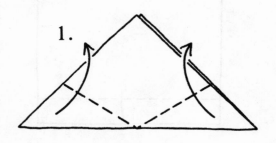

1.

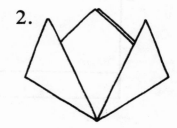

2.

Options/Uses

Stationery Decorations: If you like, you can design your own emblem to suit your personality by selecting another of the paper-folds in the book. Not only completed figures, such as the penguin, but some intermediate folding steps can become abstract forms. Use them singly or combine several into a decorative design.

On most of my letters I stick a simple flower to convert a typed or word-processed letter into a personal greeting. It only takes a minute—especially as I always keep a few folded blossoms on hand. Many recipients tell me how much this little flower brightens their day.

You need:

1½'' (3 cm) colored paper square
Glue
Green felt tip pen

1. Fold square on the diagonal. Bring outer corners up.
2. Glue flower to completed letter and draw on stem and leaves with a felt tip pen.

DOG MASK

Use a 12" (30 cm) square of paper. Follow the directions for Tulip Sticker and turn it upside down. Draw on the desired facial features.

Options/Uses

All Kinds of Masks: The pattern can be turned into almost any disguise by changing the facial features. An example is illustrated in color on page 34. To wear the mask, punch holes at the sides of the face and attach an elastic or string. Cut out circles for the eyes.

BARKING DOG

You can transform the mask into a hand puppet with two additional creases. At the beginning, fold the square on the vertical diagonal and unfold. Then proceed with the directions for the dog mask.

At the end, form a mouth by folding up the bottom corner of the front layer. Now when you hold the ears, one with each hand, and push toward the middle, the dog becomes animated. You can bark to make the head speak.

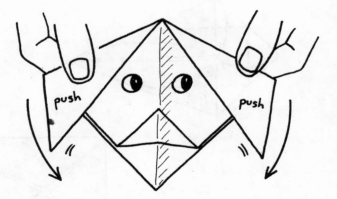

CHINESE DUCK

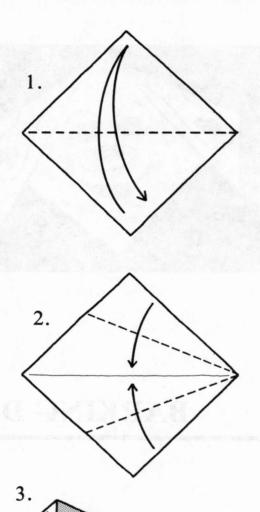

1.

2.

3.

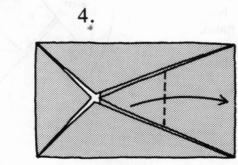

4.

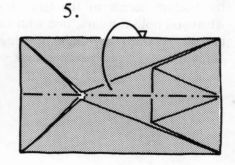

5.

For centuries the duck has been a favorite subject for Chinese artists, and a pair of mandarin ducks often symbolizes married happiness. Also Chinese boatmen, in the past, wore duck-shaped amulets to protect themselves from drowning.

Use a square about 6'' (15 cm).

1. Fold paper on the diagonal. Unfold paper flat.
2. Fold two edges to the diagonal crease.
3. Fold all four corners to meet at O.
4. Make the head by folding the point of the longest triangle to the edge.
5. Fold the paper in half lengthwise, with the head on the outside.

6. Hold the body of the duck loosely with one hand. With the other hand lift up the neck. Crease the side edge to keep it in place.

7a. Hold duck loosely with one hand and with the other hand pull the tail up and squash it flat.

7b. Hold the duck loosely at the neck and with the other hand pull the head up. Crease the back of the head.

8. Duck will stand.

8.

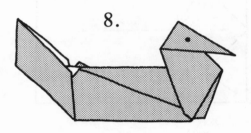

7a. 7b.

6.

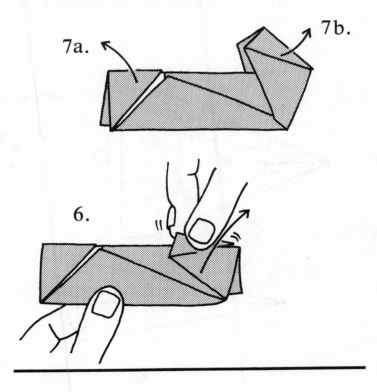

Options/Uses

Greeting Card: Fold two ducks from 3½" (8 cm) squares and glue them to a blank greeting card or a folded piece of paper. Because of the significance of ducks in Chinese symbolism, I like to send this card in response to the announcement of an engagement or to a wedding. I have often considered this a good solution when a gift seems unnecessary, but when I want to send more than an ordinary card. Some recipients have framed my cards.

Table Centerpiece: Fold several ducks from paper squares varying in size from 2" to 3½" (5 to 9 cm). Make a duck pond by covering a round piece of cardboard with kitchen foil; cut some water lily pads from green paper and glue them on the foil.

AIRPLANE

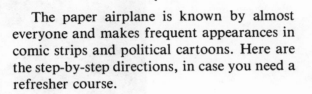

The paper airplane is known by almost everyone and makes frequent appearances in comic strips and political cartoons. Here are the step-by-step directions, in case you need a refresher course.

Use an 8½" by 11" or an international size A4 sheet of note paper or stationery.

1. Fold paper in half lengthwise. Unfold paper flat.
2. At one end, fold the corners to the middle.
3. Bring the folded edges to meet in the middle.
4. Bring the folded edges to the middle. Turn the paper over.
5. Fold the airplane in half lengthwise.
6. Hold the airplane from below and let the wings spread sideways.
7. Throw the airplane at a slight upward angle.

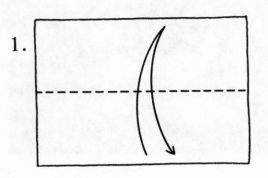

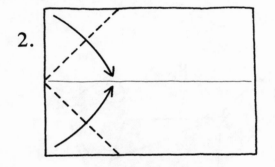

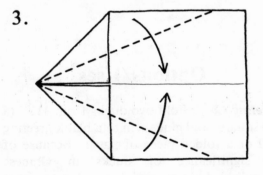

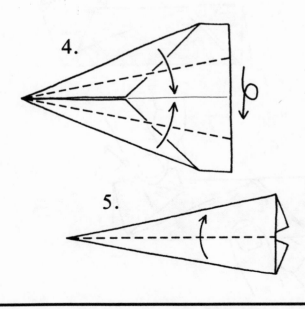

Options/Uses

Party Game: At a party have all the guests make airplanes according to the instructions, or with changes. Establish rules as to whether paper clips are to be allowed to weight the nose, cellophane tape to hold the plane together, and felt tip pens to decorate the craft. Then have a contest to see whose airplane can fly the longest distance, the highest, the swoopiest. Invent other winning categories. Not only children enjoy this game!

MONSTER PUPPET

The monster puppet responds to requests from elementary school teachers and others who have asked for something very simple. Even if the folding is not done very accurately, children will still end up with a workable puppet. Almost any kind of rectangular paper is suitable, even a page from a magazine or computer paper.

Use an 8½''x11'' or international size A4 sheet of paper.

1. Fold paper in half the short way.
2. Fold paper in half again.
3. Fold paper in half backward (Mountain Fold).
4. Fold two edges to the crease just made.
5. Paper now has two pockets. Insert two fingers into one pocket and the thumb into the other. Make the puppet talk by moving fingers and thumb apart and together again.

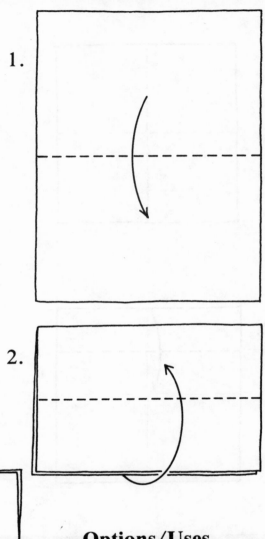

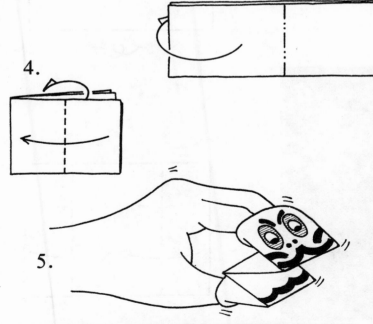

Options/Uses

Decorations: Draw on facial features with crayons or felt pens. Glue on small paper cut-outs for eyes, tongue and other decorations. Turn the puppet into almost any character: animal, superhero, monster, parent, teacher or friend.

For Young Children: For very young children make smaller puppets from sheets of paper cut in half.

Big Mouth: Make a wide-mouthed puppet by folding the paper lengthwise in step 1. Then proceed as before.

HOUSE

1.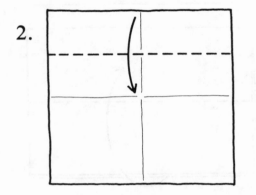

Even very young children delight in making this house.

Use a square about 6'' to 8'' (15 to 20 cm).

1. Fold paper in half in both directions. Unfold paper flat.
2. Fold top edge to the center crease just made.
3. Turn paper over.
4. Fold side edges to the middle.

2.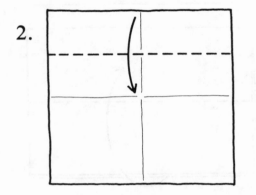

3.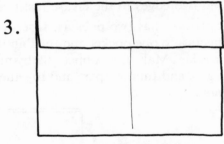

4.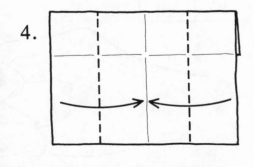

5. Slide your finger under the little square flap at the top. With the other hand bring the corner marked X to the outside. Then squash the roof flat. Look at the next drawing. Repeat with the other side.

6. House stands up, if sides are placed at right angles to the front.

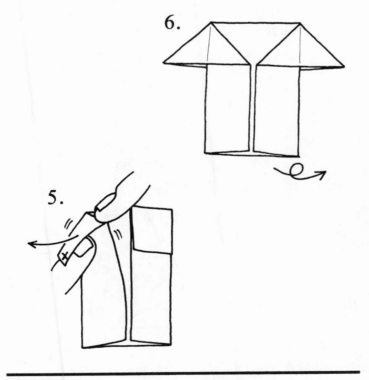

Options/Uses

Doll House: Make a large doll house by cutting a 12" (30 cm) square from a grocery bag.

Diorama: Have children build their own town by making several houses, placing them on a large piece of cardboard, drawing roads, and adding trees and other landmarks. They can pretend to visit friends or relatives, and they will invent games of their own.

Greeting Cards: You can write your message directly on a folded house or you can glue a smaller house to a piece of folded stationery. This is a charming idea for inexpensive invitations to an "Open House" or as a change-of-address notice when moving.

PENGUIN

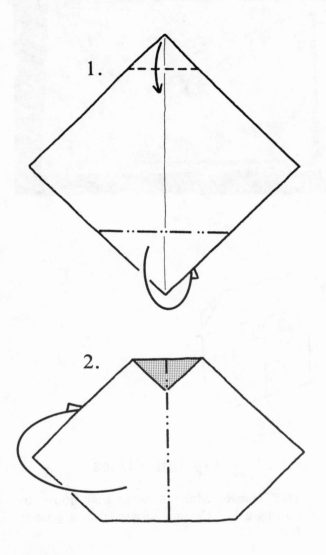

1.

2.

3.

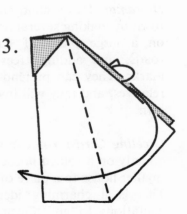

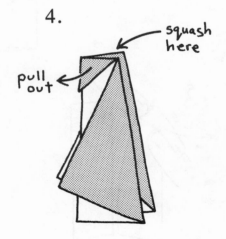

4.

squash here

pull out

This penguin is created with only a few folds and is most effective when made from paper that is black on one side and white on the other. This feature can be found in origami and gift wrap papers but, if these are not available, black paper can be used. Black paper can also be backed with white paper by pasting the sheets together.

Use a paper square about 6'' (15 cm).

1. With white side of paper up, fold square on the diagonal. Unfold paper flat. Fold the top corner down about 1'' (2.5 cm). Fold the bottom corner back about 2'' (5 cm).
2. Fold paper in half backward (Mountain Fold).
3. Bring outer corners over beyond the edge, first on the front, then on the back.
4. Pull head forward and squash the back of the head flat.

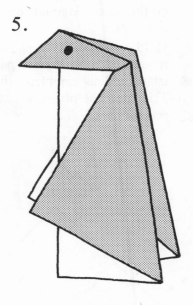

5.

Options/Uses

Penguin Family: Two large and several smaller penguins can be arranged as wall pictures, greeting cards, or figurines, and such arrangements are also effective in dioramas of arctic scenes.

Children's Party Decorations: For table decorations make penguins from 10'' (25 cm) paper squares, or other sizes if you prefer. Use 22'' (55 cm) squares of sturdy paper to make giant penguins to stand on the floor.

THE SURPRISING TRIANGLE

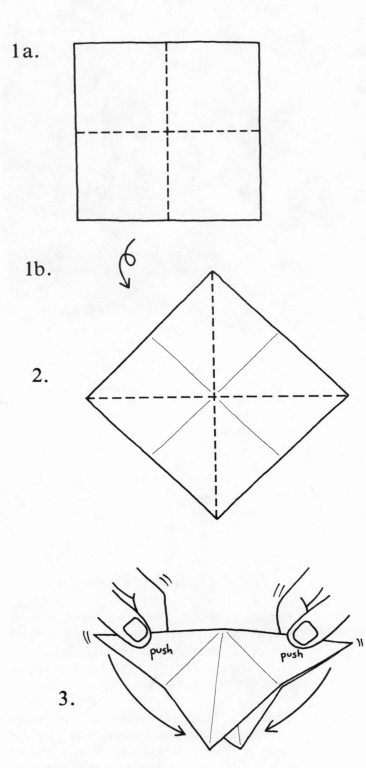

1a.

1b.

2.

3.

The things on the next few pages are all made from a simple, folded triangle. Hang it and you will have the String-Up; turn it sideways and you will have a Star. Combine several units into a tree for a greeting card or an Executive Toy.

In paperfolding jargon this triangle is called the triangle (or waterbomb) base, which forms the beginning of many other projects. Because of its versatility you can also call it a module.

Use a square about 4'' (10 cm).

1a. With colored side of paper up, fold square on broken lines shown.

1b. Turn paper over.

2. Fold on the diagonal. Unfold. Fold paper on the other diagonal, but do not unfold this time.

3. Hold paper exactly as shown. Push hands toward each other until paper forms a triangle. This completes the Surprising Triangle. The projects that follow show several uses.

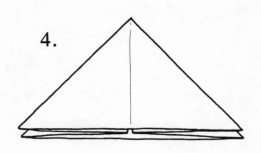

4.

SEASON'S GREETINGS

For this greeting card make three triangles in graduated sizes from 1½'', 2'' and 2½'' (5, 6 and 7 cm) squares. Glue them on a blank greeting card.

Options/Uses

Quilt Designs: Glue several triangles into stars and other geometric quilt-type patterns. The results are three-dimensional, as opposed to using plain, cut triangles. Like quilts, you can use them as wall pictures, or make more greeting cards.

EXECUTIVE TOY

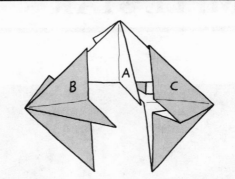

This is fun to look at, or treat as a puzzle or holiday ornament. It's made from six Surprising Triangles that are interlocked. The procedure requires too many drawings and I hope the single drawing allows you to catch onto the trick. As many engineers and mathematicians are intrigued with this construction, I am including it as a paperfolding challenge, in spite of the sparse instructions.

Choose three different colors and make two Surprising Triangles in each color. Slide two opposite corners of unit A into the corners of units B and C. Slide the corners of two other units into the uncovered corners of unit A. Continue interlocking all six units by alternating covered and uncovered corners.

TRIANGLE STRING-UP

You need:

Square about 3½'' (8 cm)
Needle and thread
Small button (or a small scrap of paper)

Make the Surprising Triangle.

Thread a needle and secure one end to a button. Then push the needle through the center of the triangle from underneath.

Before hanging the string-up, arrange the four flanges at right angles to each other.

Use String-Up singly, or cut three or more squares in graduated sizes, with one inch (2 cm) difference between them.

SIMPLE STAR

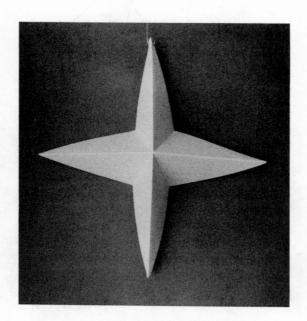

Make the Triangle String-Up but suspend it from a corner rather than from the center.

Options/Uses

Christmas Tree Ornaments: Make stars from gold and silver giftwrap foil cut into squares. Glue two squares back to back for color on both sides. You can make tiny stars to fill in those annoying gaps that often develop when you decorate a Christmas tree.

Top of the Tree: Tape a piece of wire to the lower half of the star and attach the free end of the wire to the top of the tree.

Mobile: Glue colored paper strips to the bottom of the star.

Greeting Cards—Chinese Ducks (pg. 22); Season's Greetings (pg. 31);
Tulip Stickers (pg. 20); Four Squares (Fortune Teller, drawing 2,
pg. 80); Penguin (pg. 28); Dollar Bow Tie (pg. 74); Jumping Frogs
(pg. 16).

Hats and Disguises—Top row: Cone Hat (Flower upside down), pg. 106, with two Fan Flower Quickies, pg. 50; Yellow Mask, pg. 19. Middle Row: Party Hat, pg. 52; Pink Mask (Surprising Triangle), pg. 30; Royal Blue Hat (Chinese Pagoda), pg. 42. Bottom Row: Red Visor Hat, pg. 89; Headband (Napkin Ring), pg. 105.

34

*Table Toppings—Chinese Pagoda Tower (pg. 42); Bouquet of Flowers
(pg. 106); Chinese Junk (pg. 90).*

*Mobiles and Toys—Comet Mobile (pg. 83); Balloon Flight (pg. 38);
Halloween Decoration (pg. 38); Snake (pg. 78); Finger Puppets (pg. 19).*

Amuse a child or decorate your Easter dinner table with this little rabbit.

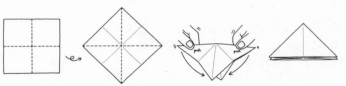

SURPRISING TRIANGLE

Use pastel colored paper about 6'' (15 cm) square.

1. Begin by folding The Surprising Triangle shown on page 30. Place it in the exact position illustrated, with two flaps on each side.

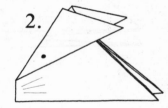

Fold the top corner of the front flap only, so that it sticks out over the long edge. Note the crease does not begin at the bottom corner, but a little higher up.

Turn paper over and fold back flap to match. Draw on eyes and whiskers.

2. Rabbit stands up.

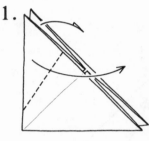

CHINESE BALLOON

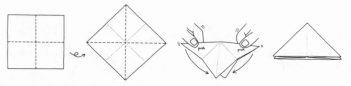

SURPRISING TRIANGLE

This ball is also called a water bomb, and its beginning triangle the water bomb base.

Use a 6'' to 8'' (15 to 20 cm) square.

1. Begin with The Surprising Triangle, drawing 4, on page 30. Place flat, with two flaps on each side. If you have three flaps on one side and one on the other, then flip one over. Fold the two outer corners up, front flaps only. Turn paper over and repeat on the back.

2. Front flaps only, bring outer corners to the middle. Turn paper over and repeat on the back.

3. Tuck the loose points at the top into the pockets of the triangles as far as you can. Crease sharply. Repeat on the back.

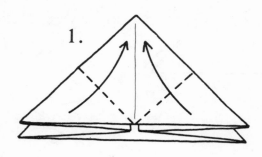

1.

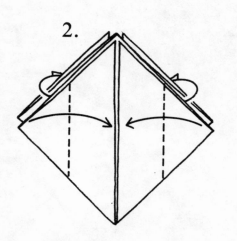

2.

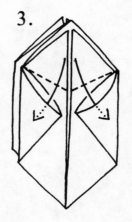

3.

4. Now inflate the ball. Slide your forefingers into the sides and hold paper together by placing your thumbs on the outside. Blow into the little hole and at the same time relax your hold so that the balloon can inflate. After inflating, you may need to shape the ball a little so that all the sides are more even.

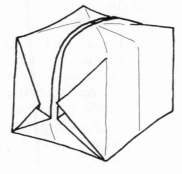

Options/Uses

Mobiles: For hanging a ball, it is best to attach the thread to the basic triangle shown in drawing 1 before you make the other folds.

Balloon Flight: Make a ball from a 20'' (50 cm) square of paper and another one for the basket from a 5'' (12 cm) square. Cut four 7½'' (20 cm) lengths of yarn. Glue them to the corners of the balls to hold the two pieces together.

Pineapple: Make a ball from a 12'' (30 cm) square of yellow paper. Cut leaves from green paper and glue them to the top of the ball.

Chinese Trick: Draw a small picture or write a word or two in the center of the square. When the ball is folded and blown up, ask someone to peek in through the hole to discover a secret message.

Photo Cube: Crease edges of a ball sharply and paste photos on the sides.

Halloween Decoration: Make a ball from orange paper and draw on a jack-o-lantern face.

4.

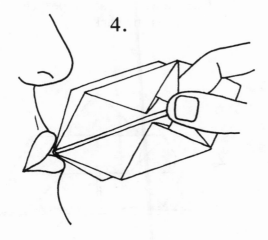

CHRISTMAS TREE ORNAMENT

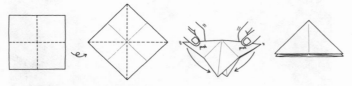

SURPRISING TRIANGLE

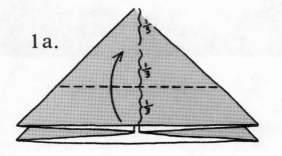

1a.

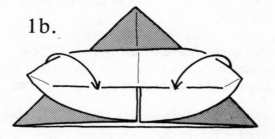

1b.

In one evening your family can make enough ornaments to cover a whole tree, for "bows" to attach to gift packages, and for decorations to brighten the Christmas dinner table.

In contrast to glass balls and ornaments made from other materials, these paper stars can be stored easily in a small space. They fold flat and can be reshaped quickly in subsequent years.

Use a square of colored paper, between 4" to 8" (10 to 20 cm).

1a. Begin with The Surprising Triangle shown on page 30, drawing 4. Place the paper flat, with two flaps on each side. If you have three flaps on one side and one on the other, then flip one over.

   On the front layer of the paper only, bring bottom edge up about ⅔ of the height of the triangle.

1b. At the same time, bring the corners toward the center, squashing them flat as shown in the next drawing.

2. Turn paper over and repeat steps 1a and 1b on the back.

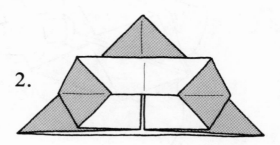

2.

3. Flip the right flap over to the left, like turning the page of a book. Turn paper over and repeat on the back, again flipping from right to left.

4. Fold front layer of paper up, as far as it will go. Turn paper over and repeat on the back.

5. Arrange the four flanges at right angles to each other, star fashion.

   Find the two "pockets" at the end of each ray of the star. Hold your forefinger in each pocket and squash the top to round the pocket.

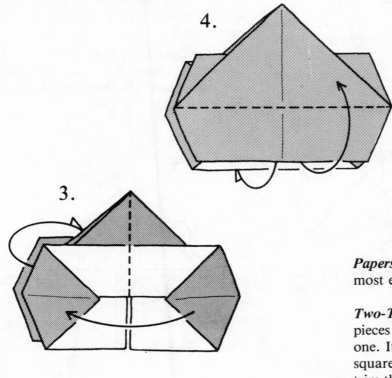

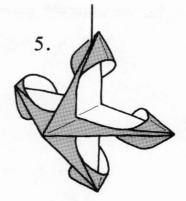

Options/Uses

Papers: Foil giftwrap paper cut into squares is most effective.

Two-Tone: For color contrast, glue two pieces of paper back to back and use them as one. It is quite difficult to glue the edges of squares together exactly even. It thus helps to trim the edges after gluing, preferably with a paper cutter.

CHINESE PAGODA TOWER

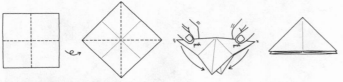

SURPRISING TRIANGLE

This many-storied pagoda consists of several similar units arranged in graduated sizes. In the typical style of the oriental structure, the rooflines of each story extend over the sides to ward off evil spirits.

You need:

6 paper squares, 4", 4½", 5", 5½", 6" and 6½" (10, 11, 12, 13, 14 and 15 cm).

1. Fold steps 1 through 4 of The Surprising Triangle, page 30. Fold the outside corners to the top corners, front flaps only. Turn paper over and repeat with the back flaps.

2. Insert a finger into the pocket on the left front. With the other hand squash down the top corner to form the small square shown in the next drawing. Repeat this with the other front flap and the two flaps on the back.

3. Fold the right front flap to the left, like turning the pages of a book. Turn paper over and again fold the right flap over to the left.

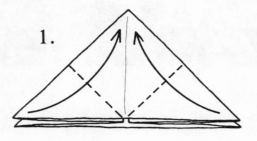

1.

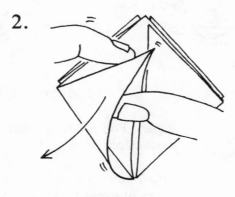

2.

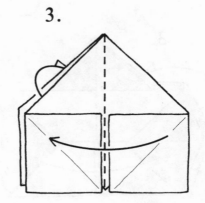

3.

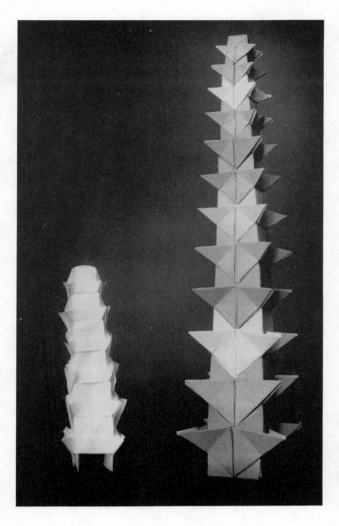

4. Fold the sides of the front flaps to meet in the middle. Turn paper over and repeat on the back.

5. Fold the right front flap to the left, like turning the pages of a book. Repeat on the back.

6. Move the single layers of paper from the middle to the sides. As you do this the bottom edge will move up. Crease into shape shown in the next drawing.

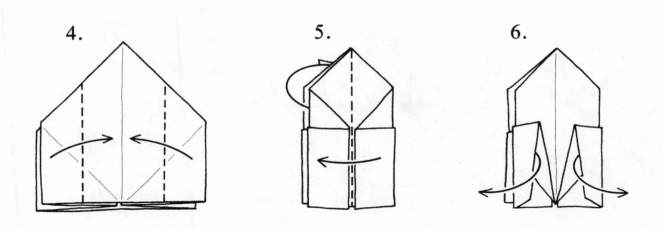

4.   5.   6.

PAGODA TOWER Cont'd.

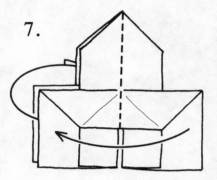

7.

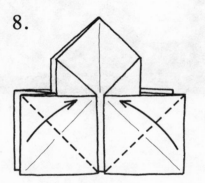

8.

7. Fold the right front flap to the left, like turning the pages of a book. Repeat on the back.

8. Fold the bottom outside corners to the middle, on the front and the back.

9. Open the pagoda by inserting a finger into the bottom and pushing out the sides. Squash down the top to form a soft square.

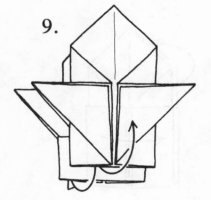

9.

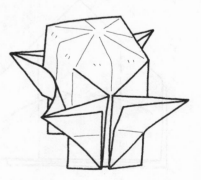

Options/Uses

Suitable Papers: Origami paper, construction paper, or giftwrap paper with small patterns all make elegant pagodas.

Two-Color Scheme: For a striking effect make each unit by placing two squares of paper in different colors back to back and using them as one. Occasionally you can find paper colored on both sides. This gives the same effect and is easier to handle.

Skyscraper Pagoda: You can make taller pagodas by stacking 12 graduated units. Reinforce the bottom section of the completed pagoda with cardboard to make the pagoda stand firmly. Making the separate pieces is a good group project for youngsters.

Table Decoration: The pagoda makes a dramatic dinner table decoration. Red and gold best suit an oriental theme, as red is the color of good fortune and gold represents wealth.

Hat: A pagoda unit folded from a 22'' (55 cm) square makes an adult-size hat.

WING-DING

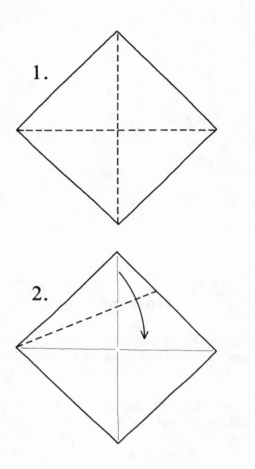

It could be a bird, a moth, a bat or whatever you like. Anyway, it flaps its wings and is entertaining.

Use a square about 6" to 8" (15 to 20 cm).

1. Fold paper on both diagonals. Unfold paper flat again each time.
2. Fold top edge to the diagonal crease.
3. Unfold paper.
4. Fold other top edge to the diagonal crease.
5. Unfold paper.
6. Pinch top corner between thumb and forefinger and let paper settle into previous creases. Flatten the pinched corner to the right. See next drawing.

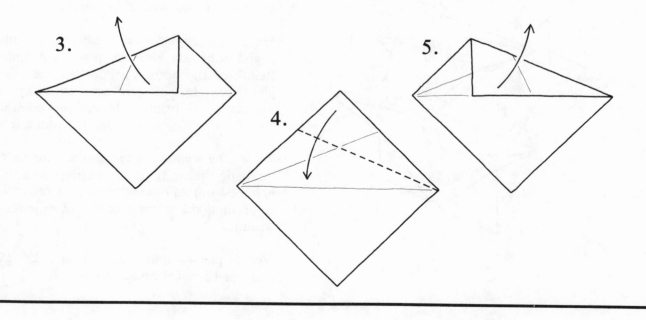

7. Fold bottom point to top point.

8. Fold top layer of paper down again, but overlapping the bottom edge.

9. Fold the right flap over to the left, backward (Mountain Fold), but do not touch the triangle shown shaded.

10. Place Wing-Ding with the shaded triangle down as shown in the drawing.

To flap the wings, hold at 0 and pull the tail.

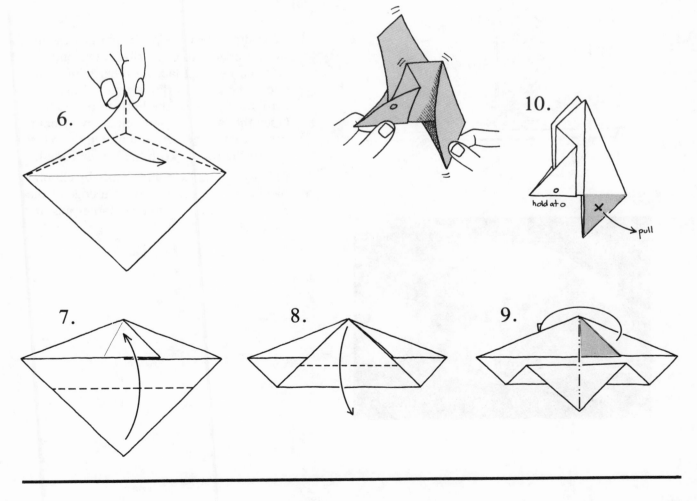

6.

10.
hold at o
x
pull

7.

8.

9.

FIREPLACE FAN

A large accordion-pleated fan is a good camouflage for a gaping fireplace during the warm months. In the winter, when the fireplace is in use, collapse the fan and store it flat.

1.

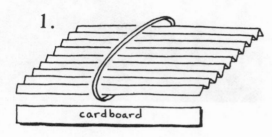
cardboard

2.

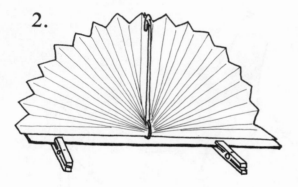

You need:

White heavy rag paper (or paper that is similar) 24'' by 36'' (60 x 90 cm)
A strip of cardboard, 24'' by 2'' (60 x 5 cm)
2 spring-type clothespins
1 large paper clip
1 rubber band
Glue

1. Accordion pleat the paper parallel to the shorter edge into eight ribs approximately 2'' (5 cm) wide. Place a rubber band in the middle or tie with thin string. Glue the cardboard strip to the bottom of the fan. Open the fan into a semi-circle by bringing two corners together, and attach the paper clip to the top to keep the fan extended.
2. Balance the fan to stand firmly by clipping two clothespins to the bottom edge at the back. For storage, remove clothespins and paper clip.

Options/Uses

Accordion Pleating: To make even pleats I recommend folding the paper in half, and in half three more times. (As the paper becomes too bulky after the second time, do not fold all layers at the same time, but fold half the packet forward and the other backward.) Open the paper flat and refold back and forth on the existing creases before arranging alternate accordion pleats.

Sizing: The suggested width of 24" (60 cm) results in a fan 24" (60 cm) wide at the bottom. You can produce other sizes by using a larger or smaller paper. Always use paper in the proportion of 1 x 1½, the smaller dimension to equal the final width of the fan at the bottom.

If available sheets of paper are not large enough, combine two or more pieces. Overlap the edges of two sheets of paper approximately 1" (2 cm) and paste them together, using glue sparingly. To be less visible the glued seam should be placed parallel to the shorter edge.

Suitable Papers: The white paper suggested in the instructions is long-lasting because of its high rag content. It can even be wiped off with a damp cloth. Many other papers can be used, including wallpaper, sturdy giftwrap, and paper selections from art supply stores.

Colors: Select colors to co-ordinate with a room's decorating scheme. Striped paper will repeat the curve at the top of the fan, if the stripes are folded parallel to the shorter edge.

When using paper colored on one side only, make sure the outsides of the first and last pleats are colored.

Doll House Fan: Make a small fan to fit a doll house from a 3" (7 cm) square of paper. The fan will stand without clothespins.

Christmas Tree Ornments: Make fans from 4" x 6" (10 x 15 cm) pieces of paper. Choose double-sided giftwrap or glue two pieces of foil giftwrap back to back.

Napkin Fan Flair: Fold fabric or paper napkins into fans and place them in stemmed glasses for a spectacular effect.

FAN FLOWER QUICKIES

Options/Uses

Giant Rounds: You can decorate large halls quickly and inexpensively by making huge patterned circles with large pleated sheets of art paper. Always begin with paper in the proportion of 1 x 2½. After pleating you can add to the form by cutting the ends of the pleats in curves or angles.

Christmas Ornaments: Make fan flowers from 4" x 6" (10 x 15 cm) foil gift wrap.

Topiaries: Make three fan flowers in graduated sizes and attach them to a dowel stick. "Plant" them in a pot.

Accordion pleated flowers can be one of the easiest ways to create splashes of color for table decorations. The same method of folding used for the Fireplace Fan, page 48, can solve many last-minute decorating problems. By simply increasing the size, you will have flowers large enough for huge auditorium walls.

You need:

8" x 20" (20 x 50 cm) giftwrap.
Glue
A drinking straw
A plastic cup or other container
Kitchen foil

1. Accordion pleat the paper parallel to the short edge.
2. Tie the center of the paper with a rubber band or thread. Open the fan into a circle by spreading half the pleats up and the other half down. Glue the edges together.
3. Glue the straw to the back of the pleats. Cover the container with kitchen foil. Ball up more kitchen foil and "plant" the flower in it. Use enough foil to counterbalance the weight of the flower.

POP-UP GREETING CARD

Here is an unusual greeting card, which is sure to be appreciated by the recipient.

———

You need:

2 pieces of green tissue paper, each 6'' by 8'' (15 x 20 cm)
1 blank greeting card, approximately 4¼'' by 6'' (10.5 x 15 cm)
Scissors
Glue

1. Fan pleat both pieces of tissue paper parallel to the short edges of the paper into eight ribs. Pleats are about ½' (1 cm) wide. Cut one fan into 4'' (10 cm) and 2'' (5 cm) lengths.

2. Fold all three fans in half. Glue the edges together lightly to form a semicircle.

3. Glue the semicircles to the inside of the greeting card. Cut a small green triangle and glue it near the top of the card.

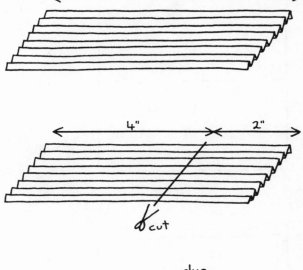

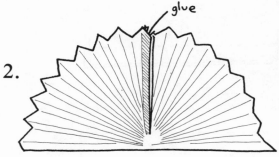

PARTY HAT

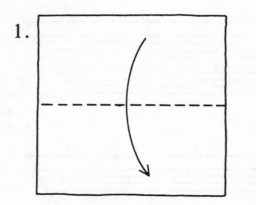

Chinese opera costume, chef's hat, or outer space headgear—this hat can parade in many different and fantastic guises.

Use a 19'' (48 cm) paper square for a child.
  a 23'' (57 cm) square for an adult.
  a 6'' to 10'' (15 to 25 cm) square for a doll.

1. Fold square in half.
2. Fold up front layer of paper only, as a cuff.
3. Fold paper in half and unfold. Turn paper over.
4. Fold outer edges to the middle.
5. On the front, fold the top corners from the middle out. Corners will stick out over the side edges.
6. Fold the bottom edges up.
7. Hat opens at the bottom.

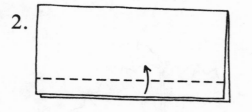

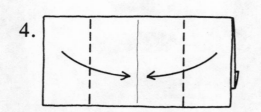

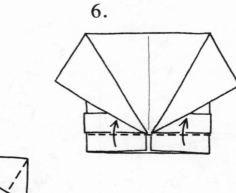

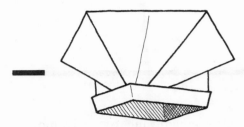

Options/Uses

Birthday Parties: Paper hats can serve the double purpose of providing entertainment and being inexpensive party favors. Give sheets of paper to children and guide them step-by-step in making their own hats. Let them decorate the hats with felt tip pens and stickers.

Costuming: Teachers and parents can arrange to costume a whole play with these hats.

Greeting Card: Make an all-occasion greeting card by pasting a doll-size hat to a piece of stationery or folded piece of construction paper. The message? "My hat's off to you..." on your graduation, on your birthday, on your promotion.

Place Cards: Use doll-size hats as place cards.

Papers: Any kind of paper available in large sheets can be turned into hats: newspaper, especially the comics pages, white newsprint, giftwrap, brown kraft paper, leftover wallpaper, and paper selections from your local art store.

Size Adjustment: If a hat is too large, you can cellophane tape the bottom edges together at one or both sides.

MAY BASKET

Make the party hat, and by turning it upside down you will have a May basket.

For a 5" (12 cm) basket use a 10" (25 cm) square of construction or giftwrap paper. You also need a strip of paper 1" by 9" (3 x 25 cm) to make a handle. Fold the strip of paper in half lengthwise and glue it to the inside of the edge of the basket.

TALKING WHALE

The whale is an amusing toy, as its mouth can be moved to open and close.

Use a square about 6'' (15 cm).

1. Fold square on both diagonals. Unfold paper flat.
2. Fold two adjacent edges to the diagonal crease. Unfold paper flat.
3. Fold the other two edges to the same diagonal. Do not unfold.

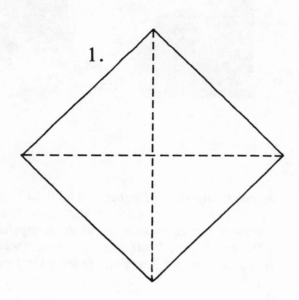

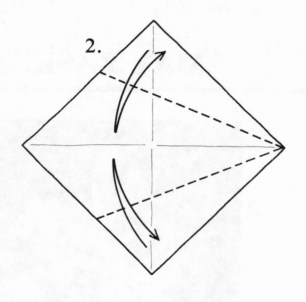

4. Fold the paper in half backward.

5. In this step two things happen at once. With your forefinger reach under corner X and bring it over to the left as far as it will go; at the same time let the edge of the paper move toward the middle on the existing crease. Repeat with corner Y.

6. To operate the toy, hold each side of the tail with one hand and move your hands apart.

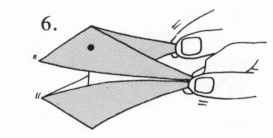

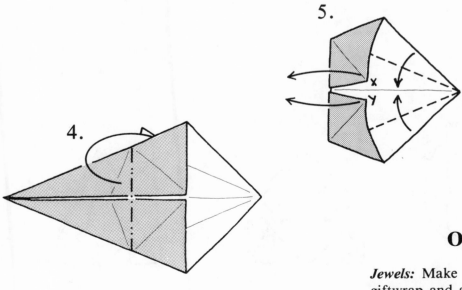

Options/Uses

Jewels: Make whales from jewel-toned foil giftwrap and suspend from the "tail" as a mobile or Christmas ornament.

EARRINGS

You can make these earrings in [...]
even two-tone and most people wil[...]
guess they are made with paper. [...]
fund-raiser.

You need:

Two 1½" (4 cm) squares of paper
White glue
A straight pin
A pair of wire fittings for pierced ears

Fold both squares in the same way.

1. Fold square on both diagonals. Unfold
   paper flat.
2. Fold two opposite corners to the center.
3. Fold paper in half backward.
4. Fold as shown by broken lines and arrows.
   Turn paper over and repeat on the back.

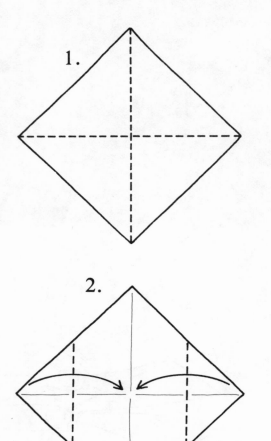

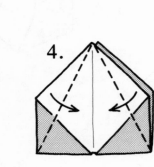

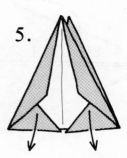

5. Pull the two corners down.

6. Glue the top corners of each earring together. With a pin, pierce a hole in the tops of the earrings for attaching the wire fittings.

6.

Options/Uses

Colors: Gold or silver foil giftwrap imitates real jewelry, but the fun is in being able to make earrings to match any outfit. Any kind of colored paper, and especially origami paper, offers wide choices. As you need only small squares of paper, you can often find areas in the illustrations printed in glossy magazines that have just the right colors.

Two-Tone: Glue two pieces of paper of different colors back to back before you cut the paper to size.

Laminating: To make the earrings more durable you can laminate them with a thin layer of white glue. The glue will be transparent after it dries. You can also spray the earrings with colorless acrylic to make them more durable.

Christmas Tree Ornaments: Use earrings made from 3'' (8 cm) paper squares.

SNAPPING ALLIGATOR

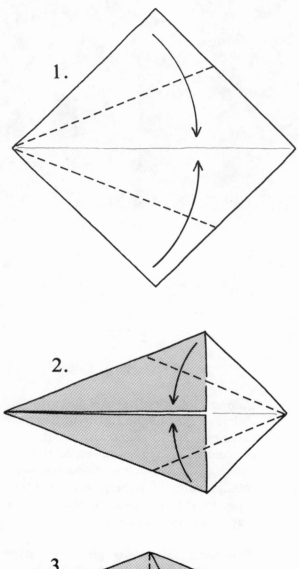

Use a square about 6'' (15 cm).

1. Fold square on the diagonal. Unfold. Fold two outer edges to meet at the diagonal crease.
2. Fold the two shorter edges to meet at the diagonal crease.
3. Fold paper in half the short way, with the extra layers inside.
4. Fold one corner to the center line, as shown by the jagged line. Unfold. Now make a reverse fold like this: Push the same corner between the main layers of paper on the creases made before, letting the paper open up temporarily. Repeat reverse fold with the other corner.

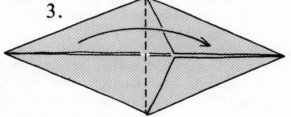

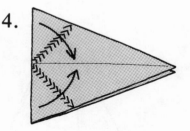

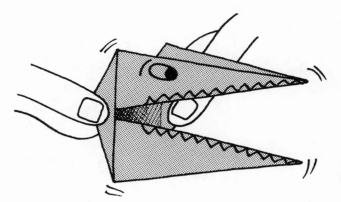

5. Fold the top layer from the bottom to the top. Turn paper over to the back and again fold the bottom layer from the bottom to the top.

6. To make the alligator snap, grasp the "ears" at the sides, one with each hand. Move the hands apart.

6.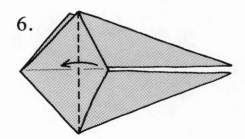

5.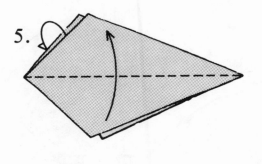

Options/Uses

Alligator Family: Children can create an alligator family by using larger squares for making the mother and father and smaller squares for the children.

Puppet Theater: Cut away the center of the bottom of a grocery box to form a frame. Place the box on top of a table and let the children stand behind it to perform stories from books or of their own imagining.

BROODING HEN

The brooding hen and the rooster, shown next, form a charming pair.

Use a square about 6'' (15 cm).

1. Start with the Alligator folded up to drawing 6, on page 58, placing it upright. Fold up the bottom, forward and backward to make a strong crease.

2. Loosen the paper and you will see a small square in the middle. Push this little square in and reform all the previous creases.

3. Make two reverse folds like this: Fold the paper down as shown by the jagged lines. Unfold. Fold again on the same creases, but this time push the folded paper in between the two main layers of paper. Let paper open up temporarily.

1.

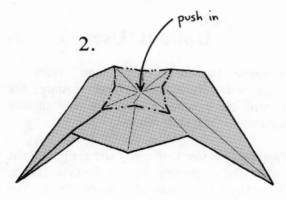

2.

push in

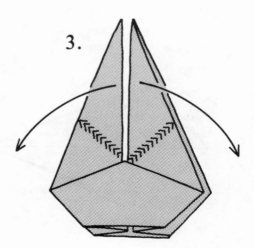

3.

4a. On the left form the tail by folding the paper down as shown by the broken line. Unfold. Open tail slightly. Then fold again on the same creases, but this time let the paper wrap round itself.

4b. On the right form the neck with a reverse fold.

5. Reverse fold the beak.

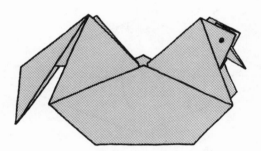

5.

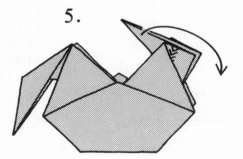

Options/Uses

Get It Right: Place paper on the drawings to help you make the right angles. Even if your paper is not the exact same size, the angles should be the same. Check the angles as you proceed from one step to the next.

Table Decorations: The brooding hen stands up well on its own. Make one for each guest. Cut white paper into small egg shapes and spread them around the sitting hens.

4.

4A   4B

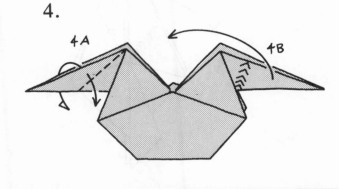

PROUD ROOSTER

This rooster is quite splendid, but before you proceed with each step, make sure your paper is facing the same way shown in the drawing. Read each direction carefully, perhaps aloud.

Use a square about 8'' (15 to 20 cm).

1. Begin with the Talking Whale shown on page 55. Fold the right flap over to the left, as shown by the dotted line.
2. Fold paper in half lengthwise.
3. On the front, fold the edge of the small triangular flap to the middle. Turn paper over and repeat the same fold on the back.
4. Fold sides up as shown by the jagged lines. Move legs aside temporarily, as necessary. Unfold. Make two reverse folds like this: Fold up on the creases you just made, but this time push the paper in between the main layers of the paper.
5. Make two more reverse folds as shown. The one on the right is higher than the one on the left.

1.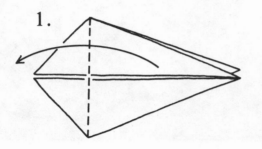

2.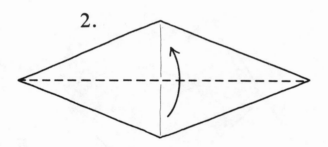

3.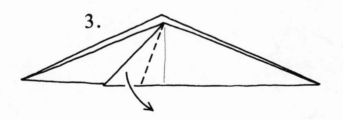

4.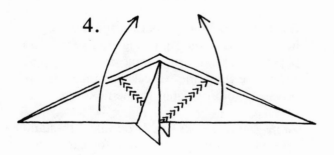

5.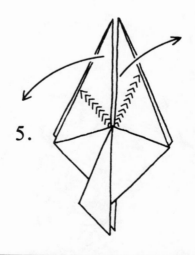

6a. Form the tail on the left: Fold the paper as shown by the broken line. Unfold. Fold again on the same creases, but this time let the paper open a little and fold the tail down and to the outside.

6b. Reverse fold again for the head which is on the right.

6c. Fold feet out.

7. And a final reverse fold for the head.

8. To make rooster stand, spread the feet apart. If he won't balance, you can glue the feet onto a piece of cardboard.

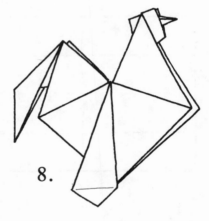

8.

7.

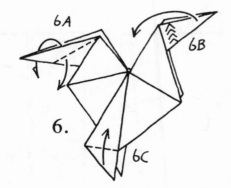

6.

Options/Uses

Get It Right: Place paper on the drawings to help you make the right angles. Even if your paper is not the exact same size, the angles should be the same.

Farmyard: Children can build a farmyard with paper roosters and hens, adding cardboard fences.

Table Centerpiece: Make an 8'' (20 cm) high rooster from a 16'' (40 cm) square of red paper. Reinforce this large rooster with pieces of cardboard cut into triangles and glued inside the legs.

Greeting Card: Glue a small rooster to a blank card.

GIFT BOX

1.

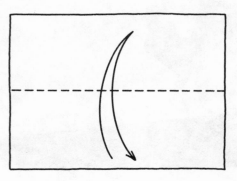

2.

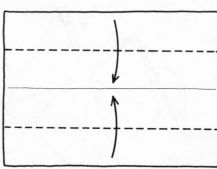

3.

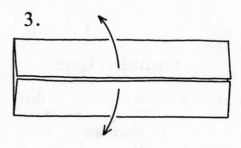

Fill it with cookies, stack it into a tower, nest it—you'll find dozens of uses for this box. If you have paper in the house, you can make a gift box in any size for rainy day toys for children.

Use a rectangle approximately 8½" x 11" or an international size A4 sheet of notepaper.

1. Fold paper in half lengthwise. Unfold paper flat.
2. Fold the long edges to the crease you just made.
3. Fold paper flat again.
4. Fold paper in half the narrow way. Unfold paper flat.
5. Fold outer edges to the middle. Do not unfold.
6. Two cut edges are in the middle with three folded lines going across. Fold each outside corner until it touches the first folded line across.

4.

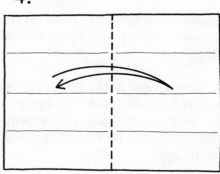

5.

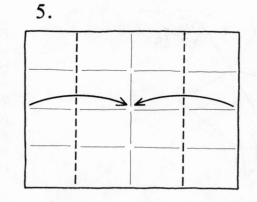

6.

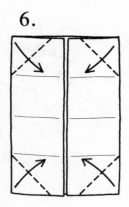

Options/Uses

7. Fold over the strips in the middle not covered by the corners.

8. Hold box at X and Y and gently pull apart. Sharpen the upright creases at the corners.

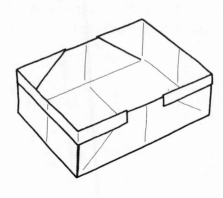

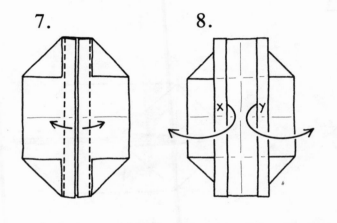

Boxes With Lids: Make two open boxes, using one for the bottom and one as the lid. If you are using typing paper, giftwrap, magazine pages, or other papers of similar weight, both pieces can be made from the same size paper.

If you are using construction paper or other similar weight paper, then the width and length of the bottom should be ¼" smaller. For example: a 9" by 12" (23 by 30 cm) paper for the lid requires an 8¾" by 11¾" (22.5 by 29.5 cm) paper for the bottom.

For smaller or larger boxes, begin with smaller or larger pieces of paper, but they must be rectangles.

You can make the boxes stronger by using paper that has been doubled or by cutting a piece of cardboard to the size of the finished box and placing it in the bottom.

Children's Toy: Make closed boxes in graduated sizes for stacking into a tower or nesting into each other.

Surprise Package: Make several nesting boxes and place the gift in the smallest before inserting each box into the next larger one.

Basket: Cut a strip of paper and attach to the edges of the box. Make small baskets for nut cups and candy dishes.

PIG

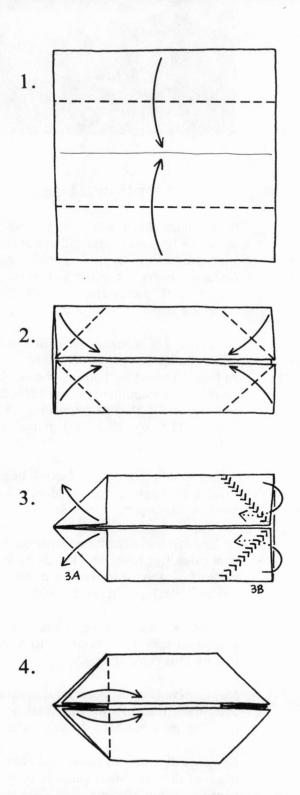

Use paper about 6'' (15 cm) square.

1. Fold square in half and unfold. Fold top and bottom edges to the crease just made.
2. Fold all four outside corners in.
3a. Unfold the four corners...
3b. and tuck each corner in between the two main layers of paper on the existing creases.
4. Flip over two corners on existing creases.
5. Fold paper in half lengthwise backward.

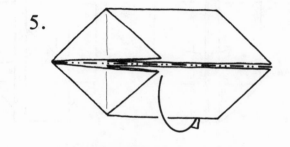

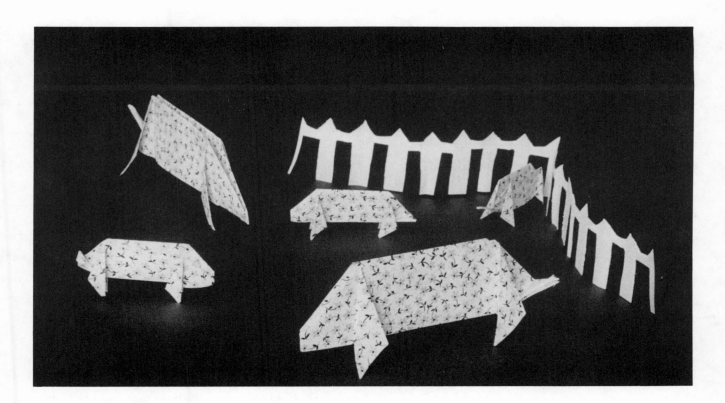

6. Make two legs on the front and two legs on the back, by folding as shown.

7. Tuck in snout and twist tail up.

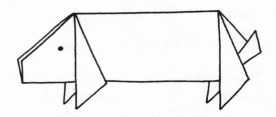

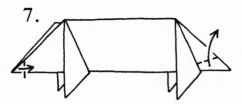

Options/Uses

Pig Family: Create a barnyard scene by making a family of pigs, adults from 6'' (15 cm) squares and children from 3'' (8 cm) squares.

Greeting Cards: Pigs can be glued to an appropriate background for a greeting card.

KITE

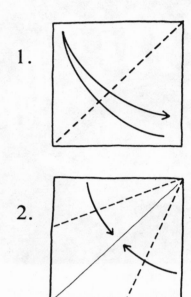

1.

2.

Options/Uses

Paper: Notebook, 8½" x 11" typing or printing papers, or international size A4 sheets of notepaper make excellent kites. Cut them into 8½ " squares.

Tail: Flight performance can be improved by weighting the kite. Glue a tail made from ribbon or paper strips to the wider end of the kite.

Variations: I saw children fly dozens of these kites while I was vacationing many years ago in the Bahamas, and soon afterward I published the directions. Since then, other paperfolders have developed some variations. I mention this to encourage you to experiment with the folding procedure of the basic kite.

Decorations: Brightly colored kites seem to paint the sky.

Notepaper or Bookmarks Paste a miniature kite on a sheet of notepaper or a blank bookmark and draw on a colorful tail.

This simple diamond-shaped kite actually flies, but with the pointed end up, which is upside-down from the way a traditional kite flies.

You need:

A square about 8" (20 cm)
Scissors
Thread or thin kite string

1. Fold square on the diagonal. Unfold.
2. Fold two edges to the crease you just made.

3. Knot a 10" (30 cm) length of thread to one inside corner. Knot a long piece of thread to the other inside corner. Knot both pieces together a few inches away from the kite. Hold the kite behind you with the long piece of string and run against the wind, letting the air catch in the kite to lift it up.

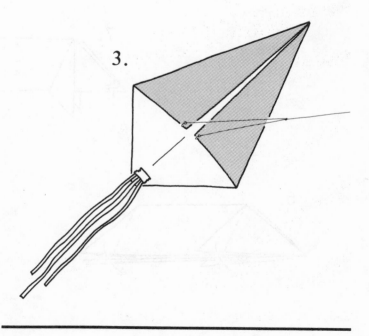

3.

Bouquet of Flowers (pg. 106) in box (pg. 88).

Decorations—Crane (pg. 96); Stacked Gift Boxes (pg. 64) with Pine Tree Ornament (pg. 107); Christmas Tree (pg. 30); blue and gold Christmas Ornament (pg. 40); Hanukkah Box (pg. 64); Wreath (pg. 79).

Use a square of silver foil giftwrap, between 2" and 6" (5 cm to 15 cm).

1. Fold square on the diagonal.
2. Fold short edges to the long edge.
3. Fold shorter edges to the long edge once more.
4. Unfold paper and fan pleat on the existing creases, alternating up and down.
5. Spread the paper apart slightly and the icicle is ready for hanging.

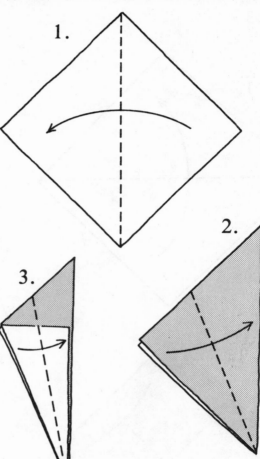

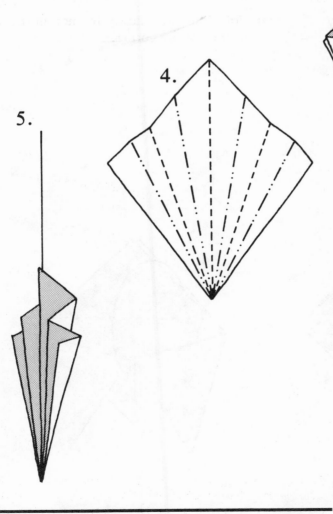

Options/Uses

Christmas Ornaments: Icicles make perfect tree ornaments and decorations throughout the house. If you would like to have color on both sides of the icicle, you can use two colored foil squares back to back and work them as one.

3-D Sunburst Picture: Make twelve icicles and flatten the center crease on each. Glue them in a circle on a posterboard for a handsome wall decoration, or greeting card if the size is small.

Rocket Mobile: Suspend several icicles from the side corner. They then resemble rocket ships in flight.

BUG

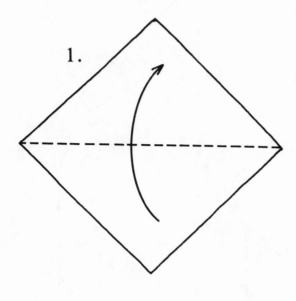

1.

Use a 3'' (7 cm) square, colored on one side and white on the other.

1. With white side of paper facing you, fold square on the diagonal.
2. Fold the two bottom corners to the top corner.
3. Fold the same corners down, leaving a small gap in the middle. Check next drawing.
4. Fold front layer down, but not all the way to the bottom corner.

2.

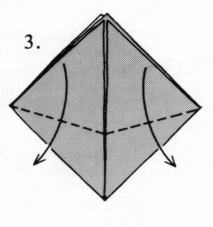

3.

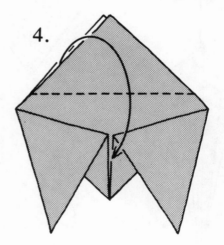

4.

5. Fold top corner down, leaving a white stripe.

6. Fold outer corners back.

6.

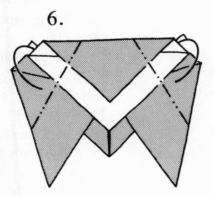

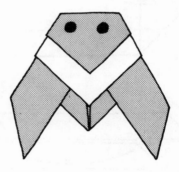

Options/Uses

Stationery: Paste one or two bugs on notepaper.

Bug Cartoon: The illustration shows two bugs holding a conversation. The "balloons" are cut from white paper, ready for writing on your message. The different appearance of the two bugs is controlled by varying the angle of the crease in step 3.

On a rainy day children can entertain themselves by making their own cartoon strips, with four panels instead of one.

Three-Dimensional Insects: Insert a finger behind the white stripe and crease bug lightly to round out its shape. Attach a thread if you want to hang any of the bugs, perhaps in giant size.

5.

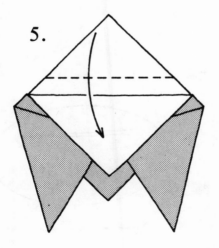

MONEY FOLD BOW TIE

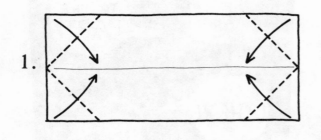

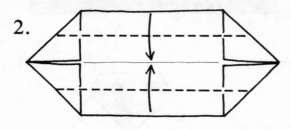

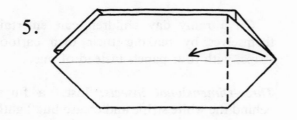

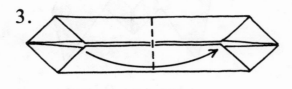

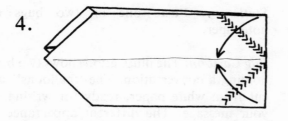

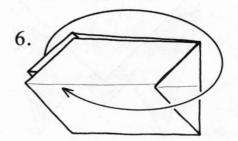

You are an instant attraction when you know how to fold a dollar bill into a bow tie. Most people watching you are especially intrigued because you are not only folding paper, you are folding money.

Use a dollar bill or a piece of paper 6'' by 2½'' (15 x 6 cm).

1. Place bill face down. Fold in half lengthwise. Unfold. Fold all four corners to the middle crease.
2. Narrow the paper by folding the edges to the middle crease.
3. Fold the paper in half the short way.
4. At the short edge fold in both corners. Unfold them, and reverse fold them in between the two main layers of paper.
5. Working at the same end of the paper, fold the small triangle over.
6. Swing the back layer of paper over to the front, hiding the small triangle inside.

7. At the short straight edge you now have four corners. Fold the two corners on the front to meet in the middle. Repeat with the two back corners.

8. Let the paper open slightly and you will see the "knot" inside. Place your thumbs on either side of the knot. At the back of the paper hold all layers of the paper firmly with your forefingers. Then gently pull your hands apart. The "knot" will expand. Release the paper and flatten the "knot" into a little square. On a one-dollar bill the picture of Washington should be in the middle of the bow tie.

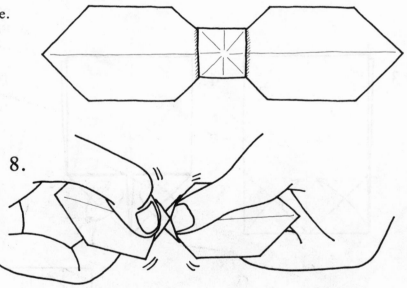

8.

7.

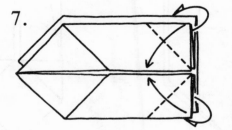

BASKET OF MANY USES

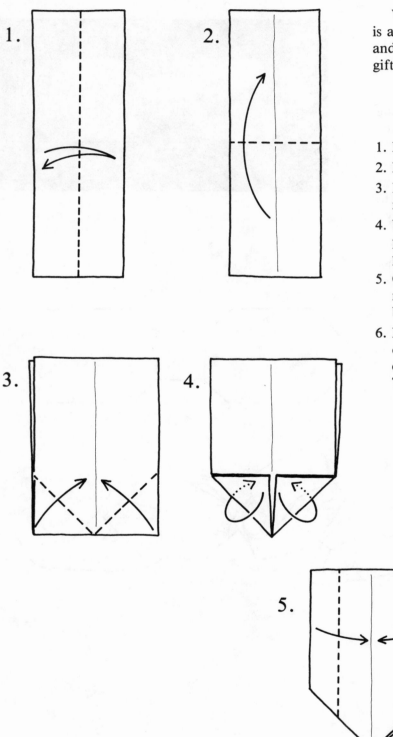

What would we do without baskets? Here is a sturdy example that is useful for parties and other purposes. Use construction or giftwrap paper 4" x 12" (10 x 30 cm).

1. Fold paper in half lengthwise. Unfold.
2. Fold paper in half the short way.
3. Bring the corners of the folded edge to meet at the middle crease.
4. Unfold corners and reverse fold them by pushing them in between the main layers of paper on the creases already made.
5. On the front, fold the outer edges to the middle. Turn paper over and repeat on the back.
6. Form the handle by narrowing the paper on the front at an angle, as shown. The edges will overlap each other at the top. Turn paper over and repeat on the back.

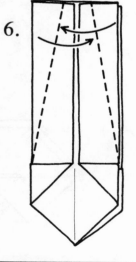

7. Fold the bottom triangle forward and back, leaving it in the same position as before.

8. Spread the handles apart and push in between them to open the bottom of the basket. Turn the basket upside down and sharpen the creases forming the bottom square. Curve handles toward each other by rolling them with your fingers. Slide the top of one handle into the top of the other. You may have to loosen one side a little.

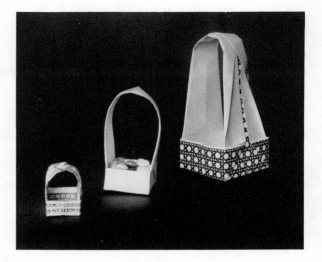

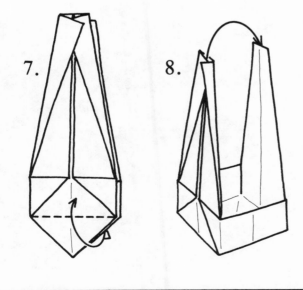

Options/Uses

Easter Basket, Gift Basket, Nut Cup: The basket can be used in many different ways depending on the size and color of paper used. Turn it into a place card by writing a name on it or gluing a small piece of paper to it.

Sizes: Always begin with a piece of paper in the proportion of 1 to 3. The size suggested in the instructions results in a basket 2'' (5 cm) wide and 4'' (10 cm) high. This size is just right for a colorful table decoration, filled with jelly beans or a mixture of nuts—also a party favor guests can take home with them.

Make a larger basket from paper 6'' (15 cm) by 18'' (45 cm). Fill the bottom with floral plastic foam and insert wired paper flowers. A charming hostess gift or table decoration.

Papers: Good quality construction paper is recommended, but sturdy giftwrap and other colored papers can be used for more dramatic effects. Use papers in two different colors back to back for a two-tone effect and increased strength.

Decorations: Glue a small paperfolded flower or animal to the top of the handle. Glue on glitter or decorate basket with felt tip pens.

Money Fold: A tiny basket can be folded from a dollar bill.

SNAKE

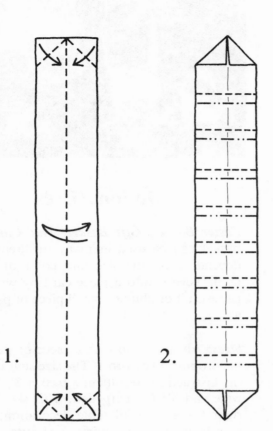

1.

2.

Children love these creepy things, and they will like the way this snake curves up and down. Use a strip of paper 2'' (5 cm) wide and at least 10'' (30 cm) long.

1. Fold paper in half lengthwise. Unfold. Fold all four corners to the crease just made.
2. Pleat the paper as shown. Fold in half again lengthwise.
3. Beginning near the head, stretch pleats at the bottom only, keeping the top pleated. Halfway along the snake, stretch the pleats at the top and keep the bottom pleated.

3.

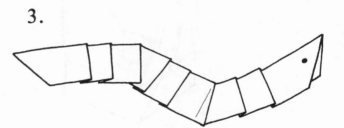

Options/Uses

Simpler Version: This reptile is not as easy to make as it looks, and it is beyond the ability of young children who lack the necessary small motor development. They can, however, make a simplified snake: Begin with the same long strip, do not fold it in half, but turn in the four corners at both ends, then simply accordion pleat it.

Variations: Once you understand the method of making unequal pleats and stretching them at the top or the bottom, you can make some variations. With wider and longer strips you can make wavy garlands. You can use pleated strips to make the arms and legs for puppets.

For a 7'' (18 cm) wreath, use small-pattern giftwrap paper 2'' x 30'' (5 cm x 75 cm). For larger wreaths, increase the size of the strip.

Follow steps 1 and 2 for the snake.

Form the wreath by stretching all the pleats at the top, keeping the bottom pleated.

Glue ends together and attach "ribbons" of paper strips.

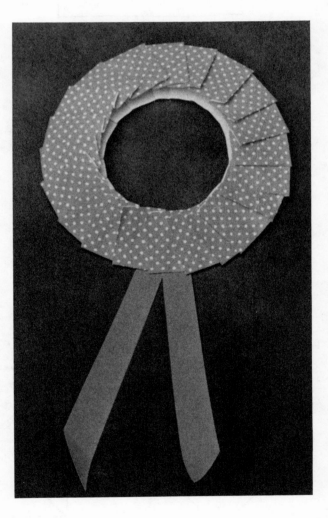

FORTUNE TELLER

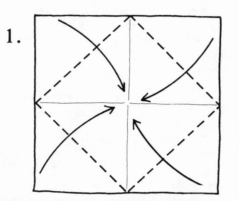

1.

If you can fold the four corners of a square to the center, you can make a Fortune Teller, a toy familiar to many people.

Use a square about 6'' to 8'' (15 to 20 cm).

1. Fold square in quarters. Unfold paper flat. Fold the four corners to the center.
2. Turn paper over.
3. Fold the four corners to the center.
4. Turn paper over.
5. Fold paper in half on the vertical backward (Mountain fold). Unfold. Fold paper in half on the horizontal backward. Leave folded.

2.

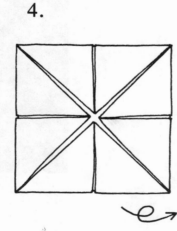

3.

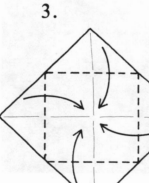

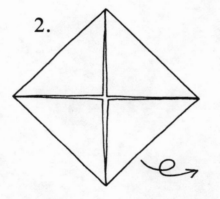

4.

5.

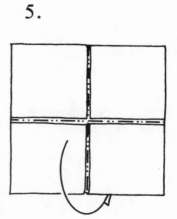

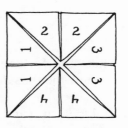

6. Grasp paper exactly as shown and push the four corners together.

7. Pull out the four small squares and reach under them by inserting thumbs into the two front pockets and forefingers into the back pockets. Move fingers back and forth, then sideways to work the fortune teller.

HOW TO TELL FORTUNES

Open the fortune teller to drawing 4. Write the numbers 1, 2, 3, and 4 on the triangles.

Lift up the triangles and write four different predictions underneath. Here are some examples:

"You will become a famous baseball player."
"You will become an astronaut."
"You will be rich."
"You will turn into a monster."

Form paper into fortune teller again.

Ask another person to select a number from 1 to 4. Then open and shut the fortune teller quickly several times to create an air of suspense and finally open it to reveal the desired number. Lift the flap and read the prediction.

Some people may know other ways to use the fortune teller, because many variations exist.

7.

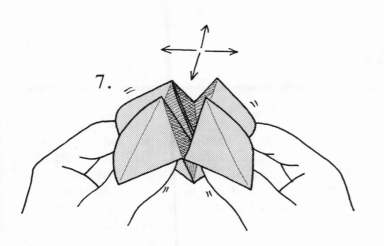

6.

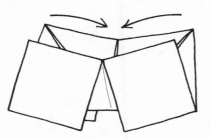

Options/Uses

Hanukkah Mobile: Make six fortune tellers from blue paper. Glue them side-by-side into a circle. The inside becomes a six-pointed Star of David.

81

CANDYDISH

Make the fortune teller and turn it upside down. You now have a candydish, sometimes called a salt cellar.

Space Rocket: Make the fortune teller and suspend it from one of the outside corners.

Comet Mobile: Glue four candydishes together into a ball-shaped star. Add paper strips to the bottom. Thread the top of the star to hang it.

Quickie Decorations: Make large candydishes from brightly colored construction paper. Attach them to dowel sticks and display them in a vase or other container.

MERRY-GO-ROUND

For a children's party make a table centerpiece. Push a 12'' (30 cm) dowel stick through the center of a pint container turned upside down. Anchor stick inside a small block of plastic foam. Cover container with giftwrap. Make a candydish from a 12'' (30 cm) square of construction paper. Tape stiff wire to the four bottom corners of the candydish. Attach four paperfold animals to the free ends of the wires. Place the candydish assembly on top of the stick. It can be moved around gently, like a merry-go-round.

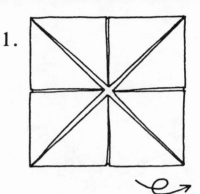

1.

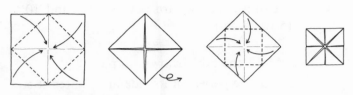

FORTUNE TELLER

Use a paper square about 6'' to 8'' (15 to 20 cm).

1. Start with the Fortune Teller drawing 4. Turn paper over.
2. Fold the four corners to the center.
3. Unfold paper to look like Fortune Teller drawing 2.
4. Pinch each of the four corners together tightly, upward. Then push the sides together to meet in the middle. Turn paper over and crease edges of the table top sharply. Table is ready to stand up.

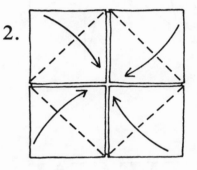

2.

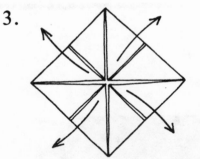

3.

4.

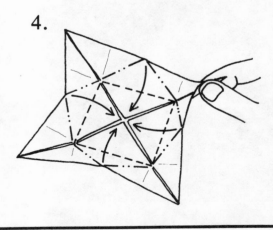

CATAMARAN [DOUBLE BOAT]

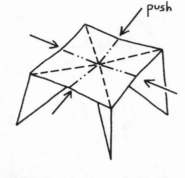

Use a paper square between 6'' and 10'' (15 to 25 cm).

1. Make the table shown on page 83.
2. Lay the paper on its side and flatten it so that two flanges are on each side (see illustration).

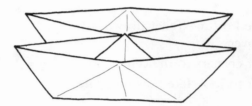

DOUBLE STAR

Use foil gift wrap cut into about 6'' (15 cm) squares. Make the catamaran. Arrange the four flanges at right angles to each other. Crease sharply.

Make the Catamaran and rotate all four corners in the same direction, as shown in the illustration. Stick a straight pin through the center of the pinwheel and then into a straw. Allow enough space between the pinwheel and the straw for the pinwheel to turn. For safety, crush a small piece of kitchen foil over the point of the pin and attach the foil securely with a drop of glue. Blow into the pockets of the pinwheel to make it turn.

Options/Uses

Giant or Mini: You can make huge pinwheels to decorate large halls or small ones for earrings or greeting cards.

WALLET

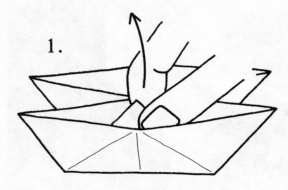

Use 6'' to 8'' (15 to 20 cm) square for practice folding. Use a 15'' (40 cm) square of giftwrap for a full-size usable wallet.

1. Place paper with colored side up and make the catamaran shown on page 84. Open the front layer slightly and pull the hidden corner of the paper into position shown in the next illustration. If paper is caught at the sides, wiggle it free. Turn the paper over and repeat the step on the other side of the boat.

2. Fold the three corners to meet in the middle, first on the front, then on the back.

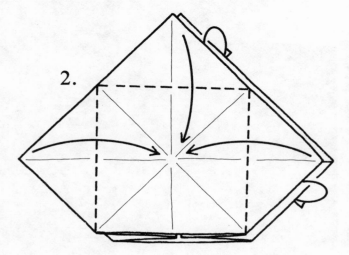

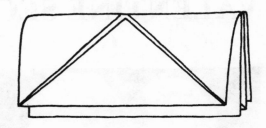

3. Fold the front flap down. Turn paper over and repeat on the back.

4. Bring back flap over to the front.

3.

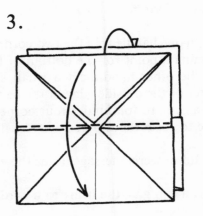

4.

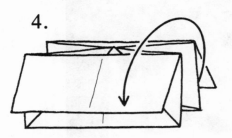

Options/Uses

Gift: The wallet can be turned into an unusual greeting card, when stuffed with a greeting and/or money.

87

BOX WITH HANDLES

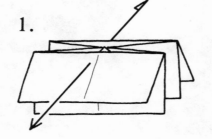

Use a square about 8'' (20 cm).

1. Start with the Wallet, shown on page 86, folded up to drawing 4. Gently pull front and back apart.
2. Lift up sides to form handles.

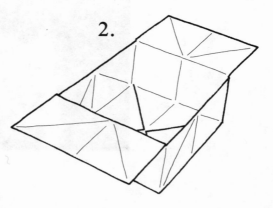

VALENTINE SECRET

Use red paper about 8'' (20 cm) square.

Make the Box with Handles. (If paper is colored on one side only, begin with colored side up.) Flatten the box so that the two handles form a square.

On one handle fold the two corners under, forming a point for the bottom of the heart. On the other handle cut a small slit at the center of the outside edge of the handle. This allows you to fold under four corners at that edge to form the top of a heart.

Hide a secret message inside the valentine.

You can glue the heart to a card and add decorations.

VISOR CAP

Use an 18'' (40 cm) square of paper.

Make the box with handles and fold one handle up.

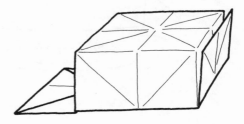

CHINESE JUNK

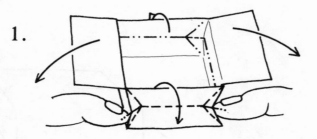

1.

2.

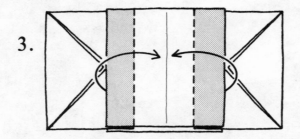

3.

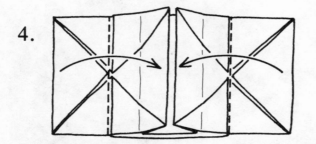

4.

5.

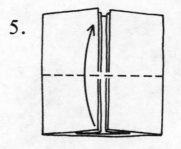

Use an 8'' (20 cm) or larger paper square.

Follow these directions carefully. Read them out loud as you go along.

1. Make the box with handles (pg. 88). Bring the middle of the lower edge to the top edge. Then push in first on one side and then on the other. Flatten. Repeat the step on the back. See next drawing for result.

2. Turn paper back to front.

3. Fold shaded areas to the middle.

4. Fold outer edges to the middle.

5. Fold in half.

6. Careful: Hold paper at the bottom on the left and pull out the right side. Then pull out the other side to the left to form the three-dimensional boat shown in the next illustration.

7. Lift and pull up the decks to form the front and back of the boat.

8. Finally, on back only, reach inside the part you have just pulled up and lift the loose corner upright.

8.

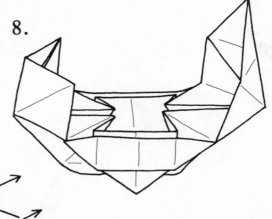

7.

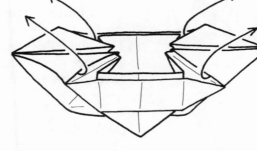

6.

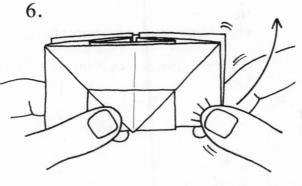

Options/Uses

Cleopatra's Barge: Make the Chinese junk from a 20'' (50 cm) square of gold giftwrap. As a final touch repeat step 8 on the front of the boat also.

Noah's Ark: The junk can be used to represent Noah's ark. Fill it with cut out or folded paper animals.

91

TELL A STORY WITH PAPERFOLDS

The Fortune Teller can be turned into animals, boxes and many other figures just by rearranging the creases. This is a wonderful visual aid for storytellers! I have made up a story called "Tyler and His Journey into Space" which includes the specific things for which directions have already been given. You can tell the same story, or make up your own.

Make the fortune teller from a 12" (30 cm) square of strong paper. Tell the story and fold the paper as indicated.

"TYLER AND HIS JOURNEY INTO SPACE"

Tyler and his mother were talking about what he'd like to be when he grew up. He decided to make a fortune teller to help him predict a profession.

(Make the Fortune Teller.)

The fortune teller said he would be a space explorer. To give himself energy for such a strenuous occupation, he took some raisins and nuts from a dish kept on the kitchen counter.

(Turn Fortune Teller upside down.)

That night Tyler had a dream about becoming a space explorer. First he entered a government program charged with building space rockets.

(Make the Space Rocket.)

He was assigned to work at a square table where three other people were already seated.

(Turn the Space Rocket into a Doll House Table.)

They talked about traveling into outer space and whether the stars would look bigger from a space rocket.

(Turn the Doll House Table into a Double Star.)

The office was near a large lake, and after work, Tyler and his three co-workers took out a boat.

(Make the Catamaran.)

When their ride was over they had to pay a small charge for renting the boat. Fortunately Tyler had taken along his wallet.

(Make the Wallet.)

The next morning Tyler told his mother about his dream and she surprised him by giving him a space helmet. Tyler put it on and said: "Can I go over to my friend's house to play? We want to explore space."

(Make the Visor Cap. Put it on yourself or on a child listener, holding the two flaps close to the head.)

Tyler's mother said: "Go ahead," and he went off. That's the end of the story.

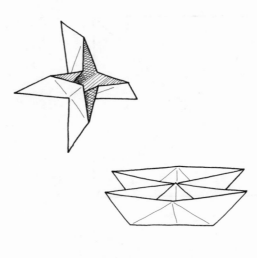

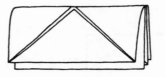

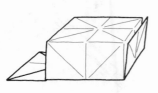

Options/Uses

Be Prepared: This story comes alive in the telling. It may seem unexciting when you read it, but try it with the props. Pre-crease the paper before you tell the story to an audience and practise making the various figures. You can use the same piece of paper for many tellings; in fact it gets better after some use.

Hidden Objects: The sequence beginning with the Fortune Teller through the Visor Cap shows how a basic pattern can produce many things by rearranging the creases, without adding any new ones. Try to find other things by experimenting with the paper.

Hands-on for Listeners: Older children can fold their own paper to illustrate the story. Even better, let them use their own imagination to make up new stories.

THE SURPRISING SQUARE

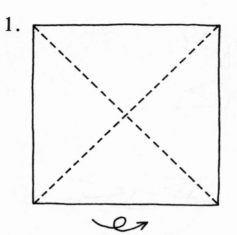

1.

The things on the next few pages all begin with a square of paper folded into a smaller square. In paperfolding jargon this is called the square base or preliminary base, because it forms the beginning of many other things. The square base by itself can be used as the center of a 3-D greeting card or as an ornament.

Use a square about 6'' (15 cm).

1. Fold square on both diagonals. Unfold paper flat each time. Turn paper over.
2. Fold paper in half and unfold. Fold paper in half the other way. Leave folded.
3. At the folded edge, grasp paper with both hands in the exact position shown in the drawing. Move hands toward each other until the paper is formed into a square. Place this flat on the table.
4. Make sure the square has two flaps on each side. If you have one flap on one side and three flaps on the other, flip one flap over. This completes the square base.

2.

3.

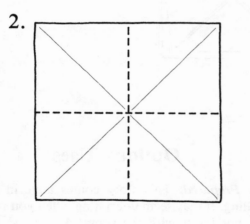

push   push

4.

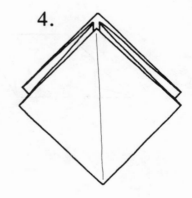

Options/Uses

3-D Greeting Card: Open the square and write your message on it. Glue the front and back of the folded square inside a blank greeting card. The message is revealed when the card is opened.

Ornament: Suspend one or more linked squares. Or glue the loose corners of two squares together.

FOXFACE TOY

Foxface is a movable puppet.

Use a square about 6'' (15 cm).

1. Make the Surprising Square base. Fold corner of top layer of paper to the opposite corner. Turn paper over and repeat on the back.
2. Grasp outside flaps, one with each hand, and move hands gently apart. This makes the Foxface Toy's mouth work.

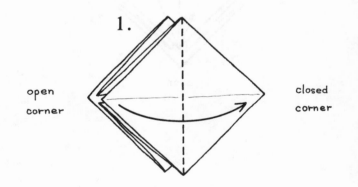

1.

open corner

closed corner

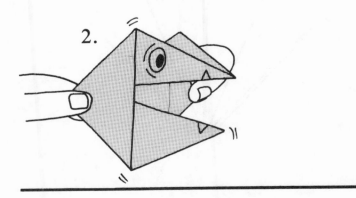

2.

Options/Uses

Gimmick: Besides the obvious attraction for children, the Foxface Toy can be used to liven up sales meetings. Make two Foxface Toys and let them hold an imaginary conversation. They can personify buyer and seller to illustrate how a salesman might respond to a buyer's questions. Similar situations in other settings may occur to you. It may just work to close a sale!

CRANE

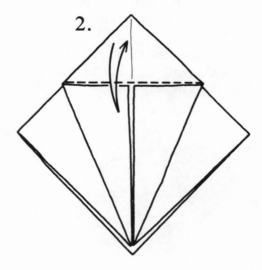

SURPRISING SQUARE

The crane is perhaps the best-known example of the art of paperfolding. Your efforts in following the steps carefully will be truly rewarded.

Use a square approximately 6'' (15 cm). If you use paper that is colored on one side and white on the other, start folding with the colored side up.

1. Make the surprising square base found on page 94. Place with closed corner away from you. Fold outer edges of the front flaps to the center crease. Turn paper over and repeat with the two flaps on the back.

2. Fold the triangle at the top forward and backward, bringing it back to its original position. This makes a helpful crease for the next operation.

closed
corner

1.

open
corner

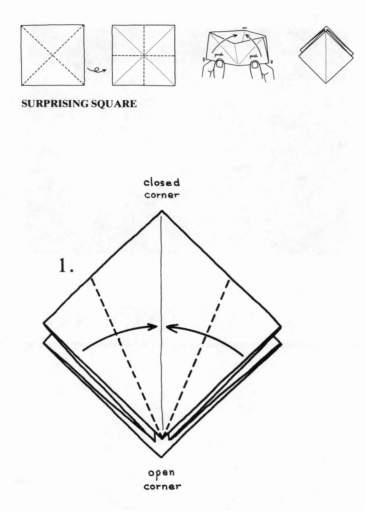

2.

96

3. Open the front flaps slightly. This exposes the corner of the paper; lift it upward in the direction of the arrow until you are able to fold the paper on the helpful crease you made in step 2. The outer edges of the paper will move to the middle as you proceed and form a diamond. Flatten the paper—see next drawing.

Turn paper over and repeat on the back.

4. This completes the "bird base," which is the beginning for many different animals.

4.

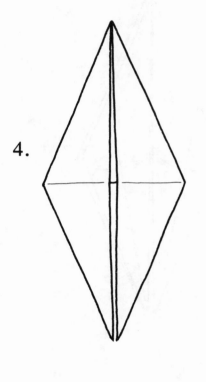

3a.

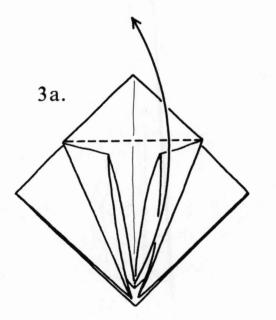

3b.

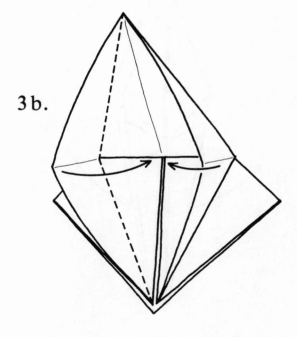

CRANE Cont'd.

5.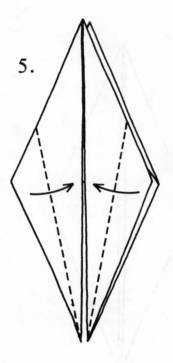

5. Fold the outer edges to the middle, first on the front flaps. Then turn the paper over and repeat on the back.

6. Make two reverse folds for the neck and tail, by bringing the two flaps up in between the two main layers of paper.

7. Reverse fold the head in between the two layers of the neck.

6.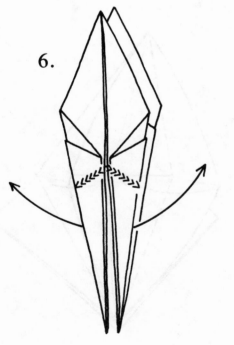

7.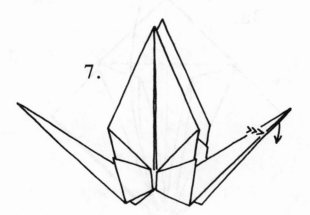

8. Inflate the crane by holding a wing in each hand. Pull gently apart and at the same time blow into the opening at X.

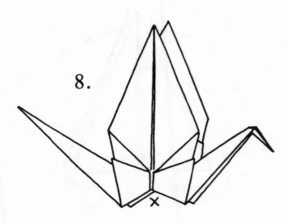

8.

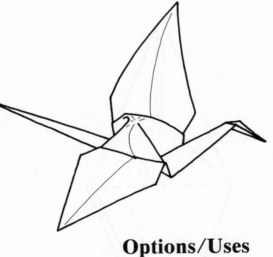

Options/Uses

Mobile: String the crane through the center point. Unfold the crane partially to make it easier. A crane can be made as large as four feet across from heavy-weight paper.

Home Accessory: Small cranes can be set on the leaves of potted plants.

BIRD WITH FLAPPING WINGS

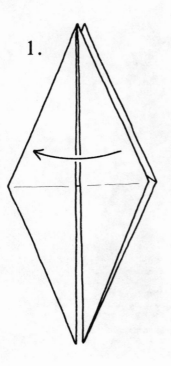

1.

This bird looks much like the crane, but the surprising movement of its wings always causes a sensation.

Use a square approximately 6'' (15 cm).

1. Make the "bird base" by following the first four steps for the crane, page 96. Fold top flap only from right to left like turning the pages of a book. Turn paper over and repeat on the back, again folding from right to left.
2. Fold bottom flap up as far as it will go. Turn paper over and repeat on the back.
3. Pull the hidden points in the direction of the arrows, one at a time. To make them stay in the position shown in the next drawing, crease sharply as shown by the broken lines.

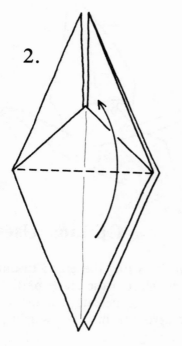

2.

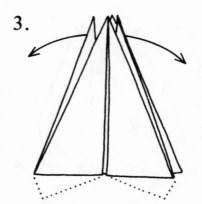

3.

4. Fold the head down in between the two layers of the neck.

5. Bird is completed. To flap the wings, hold the bird at X with one hand and gently pull tail back and forth with the other hand. Do not pull it up and down.

5.

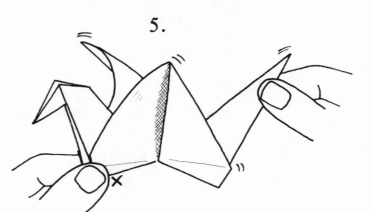

4.

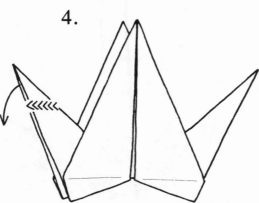

Options/Uses

Greeting Card: Glue the bird to a greeting card blank. If you use a thin coat of rubber cement, the recipient can remove the bird. Add a note to that effect with instructions on how to flap the wings.

PLEATED BIRD MOBILE

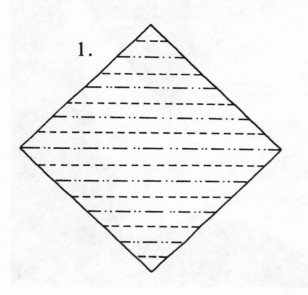

1.

This mobile swings gently in the slightest air current. And the bird's pleated wings will reflect light in changing ways if the mobile is made from light colored or foil paper.

You need:

8'' (20 cm) paper square
Needle and thread

1. Accordion pleat the square on the diagonal into eight ribs (16 creases).
2. Unfold one crease at one end. Unfold two creases at the other end. Fold paper in half, placing the corner with two unfolded creases on the outside.
3. Bend the wings outward. Spread the top of the wings. A dab of glue helps to keep the body of the bird together.
4. Attach thread to the body of the bird in two places and knot together about 3'' (7 cm) away. Leave a long piece of thread for hanging and cut off the other end of the thread above the knot.

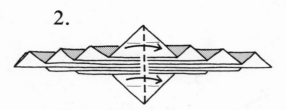

2.

3.

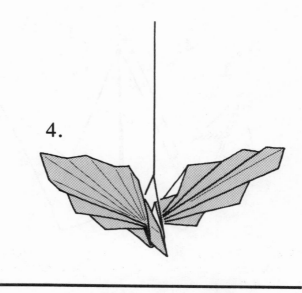

4.

Options/Uses

Baby's Delight: Make a bird in a pastel color to hang high above the crib.

Giftwrap: Cellophane tape a folded bird to the top of a stick or straw and attach the bottom to the corner of a gift box.

Children's Birthday Party—Pinwheel (pg. 84), in blue candydish
(pg. 82); Party Hat (pg. 52); Crane (pg. 96); Red Basket (pg. 76);
Napkin Ring (pg. 105).

Christmas Tree Ornaments.

These napkin rings help you coordinate the colors of any table setting, merely by choosing paper compatible with the dishes. Paper colored on one side and white on the other produces the contrasting geometric pattern.

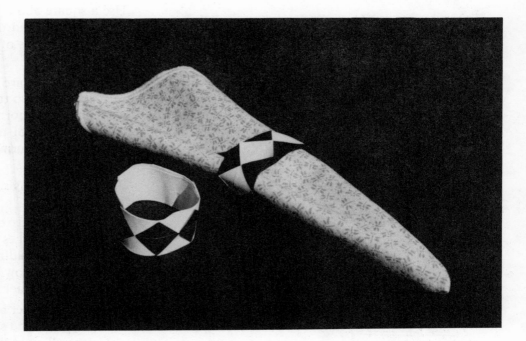

Use a 6'' (15 cm) paper square.

1. Accordion pleat the paper on the diagonal, as shown in drawing 1 for the Pleated Bird Mobile (Page 102).
2. Flatten the center crease. You then have a folded strip showing little squares.
3. Roll the paper into a circle and tuck one end into the other. You may have to narrow one edge a little. The pattern will match up perfectly, not showing any interruption. If desired you can glue the ends together.

Options/Uses

Buffets: Wrap cutlery in napkins and slide into these rings. For repeated use you can spray the napkin rings with acrylic resin or brush with urethane.

Bracelet—or Hanging Ornaments: Use 8'' (20 cm) squares of silver and gold foil to imitate precious metal jewelry.

Giftwrap Ribbon: You can substitute folded strips for ribbon.

BOUQUET OF FLOWERS

SURPRISING SQUARE

You can make a lot of these flowers quickly, ready for combining into a lasting arrangement.

Use a square about 4'' (10 cm). If the paper you use is colored on one side, start folding with colored side of paper up.

1. Make the square base found on page 94. Place square so that the four loose corners of the paper point to the top. Bring the folded edges of the front flaps to meet in the middle. Turn paper over and repeat on the back.

2. Fold top triangle down. Repeat on the back.

3. Fold the right front flap to the left like turning the pages of a book. Repeat on the back, again folding from right to left. Fold top triangle down, first on the front and then on the back.

4. Open the flower by inserting finger into the top opening and spreading the paper apart. Crease all eight vertical creases sharply.

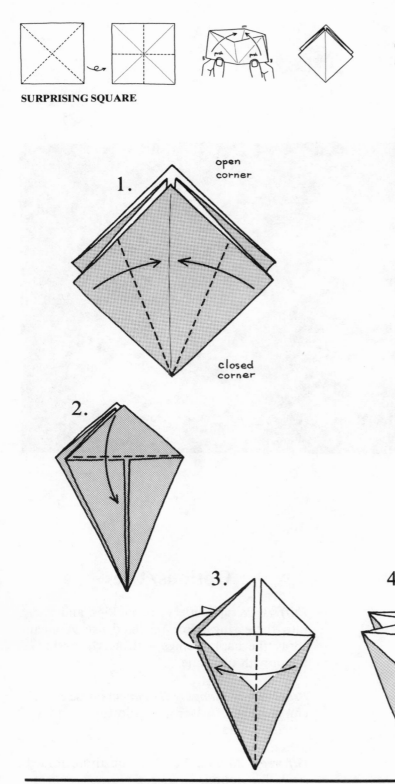

open corner

closed corner

Options/Uses

Stems: Use green covered floral wire or make stems of rolled paper. To make such a paper stem, cut a strip of green paper ¾" x 5" (2 x 12 cm). Roll it tightly on the diagonal. (It helps to make a thin stem by beginning to roll the strip over a toothpick.) Secure the end with a drop of glue. Roll the top of the stem into a loop over a pencil. Pierce a hole through the bottom of the flower and insert the stem from the top.

Leaves: Cut green paper into 2" x 18" (4 x 45 cm) strips, or any other desired length. Fold the strips in half lengthwise and glue an #18 gauge strip of wire in between the fold. Cut the long edges of the paper to shape it into long leaves.

Blooming Plants: Two or more paper flowers can be placed with live plants to give the deceptive appearance of a plant in bloom.

PINE TREE ORNAMENT

You can make a pine tree with the same folding procedure used for the flower. In the last step instead of inserting your finger to spread the paper, push in on the four central vertical lines.

The illustration shows a tree made from a 10" (25 cm) square of giftwrap, with the paper used double.

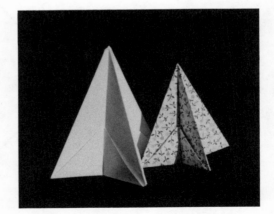

NIBBLING MOUSE

Children love this mouse, but you can decorate a party cheese tray with a family of mice and expect comments from all your guests on how clever you are.

You need:

Grey paper about 3'' (8 cm) square
Colored paper scraps
Scissors
Glue

1. Fold square on the diagonal. Unfold. Fold two edges to the diagonal crease.
2. Sharpen all three creases. Overlap the two flaps.

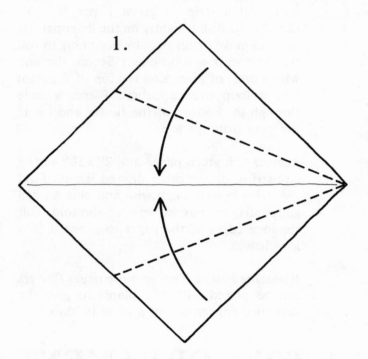

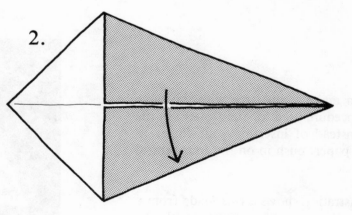

3. From the scraps, cut two ears and a strip
   about 5'' (12 cm) long for the tail. Roll the
   strip tail over a pencil. Glue the ears and
   tail to the mouse.

3.

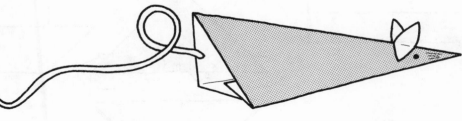

PANDA

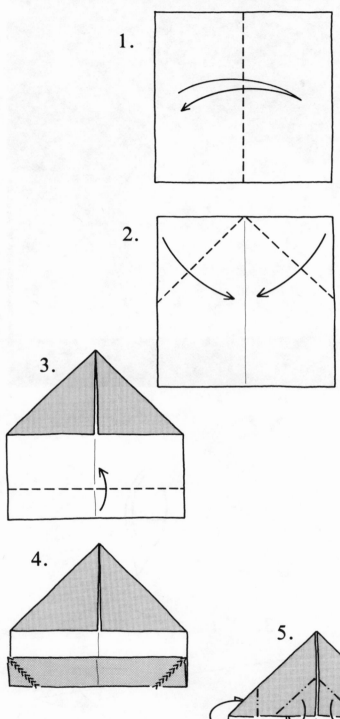

Paper Pandas on your party table, Paper Pandas in a child's room, Paper Pandas on greeting cards, they're fun anywhere.

Use two paper squares, 6'' (15 cm) or larger, black on one side and white on the other.

LEGS

1. With white side of paper up, fold paper in half. Unfold.
2. Fold upper corners to the middle crease.
3. Fold lower edge up, leaving white space showing.
4. Reverse fold both bottom corners in between the two layers of paper.
5. Fold the sides back, leaving the two bottom corners on the front untouched. Tuck the two loose corners in the middle under as shown.
6. To make the legs stand up, crease the paper in the middle and let the legs rest at a right angle to each other.

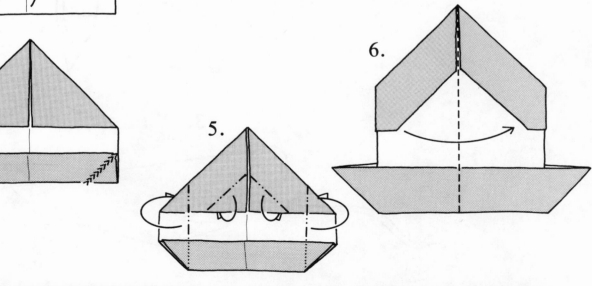

12.

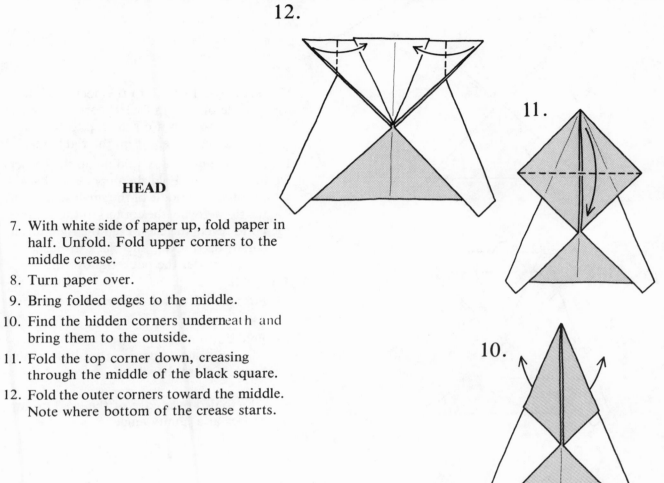

11.

HEAD

7. With white side of paper up, fold paper in half. Unfold. Fold upper corners to the middle crease.

8. Turn paper over.

9. Bring folded edges to the middle.

10. Find the hidden corners underneath and bring them to the outside.

11. Fold the top corner down, creasing through the middle of the black square.

12. Fold the outer corners toward the middle. Note where bottom of the crease starts.

10.

7.

8.

9.

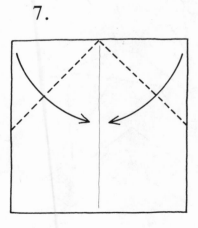

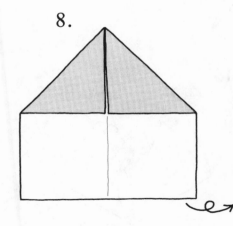

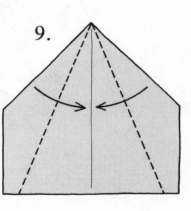

PANDA Cont'd.

13.

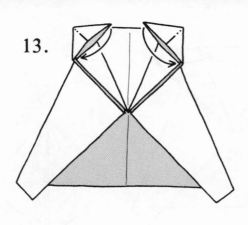

13. Poke your finger into the pocket of the triangle on the upper left corner to open it. Then squash it on the top to form a small square. Repeat on the right side.

14. Form the mouth by folding up the corner in the center. Fold the upper edge back through the middle of the small squares at the sides. Swing the corners of the squares up to reveal the ears. Fold the right lower corner up, tucking the black tip just slightly under the pocket above the mouth.

15. Fold the left lower corner up in the same way.

16. Fold bottom tip up. Then fold bottom edge up again to cover just a little of the black. Crease sharply.

Rest the folded-over edge of the head on top of the legs at a jaunty angle.

14.

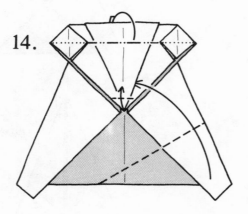

15.

16.

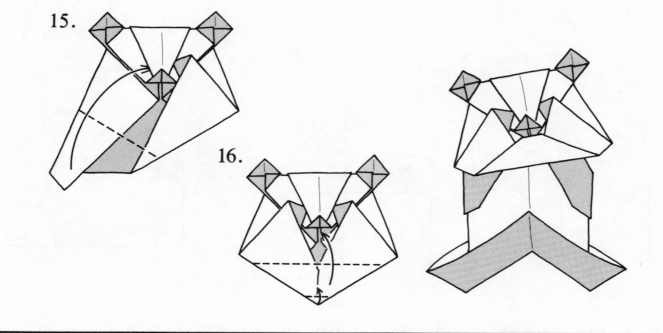

MAKE AND USE THEM

The "Options/Uses" sections throughout this book suggest ways to make good use of your paperfolds, but here are a few more ideas.

Besides obvious toys such as Jumping Frog, Talking Whale and Alligator, other paper folding projects in this book can also be turned into games for the amusement of children and adults.

Party Toys: Before the day of a party, select a project appropriate to the occasion and age of the guests. Rabbits are appropriate for Easter and holiday decorations for December. At a birthday party children enjoy Snapping Alligators and other puppets, while hats and Earrings are fun for any age. Have plenty of paper squares on hand. Show the guests how to make one or two of these favors for themselves. Children between the ages of seven and eleven really enjoy this kind of activity and often find it as entertaining as watching a hired magician.

Games: In this book folding instructions for the Airplane and Party Hat have been followed by suggestions for party competitions, but many other paperfolds can be used in a similar way. Give step-by-step directions for the Duck or the Penguin, for example, and then have a competition for making each project in the shortest period of time, or for making the largest number of such objects in, say, two minutes.

You can also provide additional paper, scissors, glue, staples, stickers, dried peas and other fixings to let the guests decorate their own foldings. Provide prizes for the most inventive, the largest, the smallest, the prettiest, and the ugliest. Develop other winning categories to give as many people as possible recognition. You'll have lots of laughs!

Toys-on-a-Stick: For small children, glue a puppet or mask to the top of a stick or straw and thus transform it into a toy that can be the beginning of a parade. Such a toy also can become a party favor.

Theater and Story Telling: The Monster Puppet, Talking Whale, Finger Puppet, Snake and Space Rocket can all be used in the puppet theater suggested for an option on the Alligator pages. Animals and objects can also be used to illustrate children's stories. Several Chinese Ducks, for example, can be used to demonstrate the well-known story, "Make Way for Ducklings". The gift box can be turned into a pirate's treasure chest or converted into a hat. The Frog Prince can court a princess made from a finger puppet. The Catamaran, Chinese Junk and Space Rocket can go on imaginary story journeys.

Party and Holiday Decorations

Almost all the projects can be converted into sparkling decorations when made from beautiful giftwrap papers or shiny paper foil. Make them in miniature or oversize as suits the occasion.

Christmas Ornaments: Nowadays all kinds of surprising things turn up on Christmas trees. The only criterion seems to be: Is it attractive, small, and light enough?

You can start a family tradition with a tree decorated from a series of paperfolds created by your family in just a few evenings. The possibilities are unlimited. Don't overlook Finger Puppets, the Wreath, Baskets, Napkin Rings and Pinwheels. You may want to use only one or two colors of paper for all the decorations or to select projects that fulfill a theme.

Simple Shapes: Some of the interim steps leading up to the final paperfolds make attractive decorations in themselves. Here are a few possibilities: Chinese Ducks drawing 3; Airplane drawing 5; Monster Puppet drawing 2 (hang from a corner at the folded edge); Ball drawing 2 (spread out flaps a little); Brooding Hen drawing 3 (upside down); Proud Rooster drawing 1; Bird Mobile drawing 2; and Bird with Flapping Wings drawing 6.

Advent Calendar: In a German tradition an advent calendar marks the 24 days before Christmas. Each day a window on the calendar is opened to reveal a hidden picture. Here is a way to make an advent calendar with paperfolds — a good school or family project.

You need 24 index cards 4'' x 6'' (10 x 15 cm). Fold them in half the short way. Glue a star or other paperfold inside. Tape the bottom edges of the cards closed with cellophane tape. Write a number from 1 to 24 on the front of each card. Glue the cards in numerical order on a large piece of cardboard in the shape of a tree. Beginning on December 1, cut the tape of the card marked 1 to open the window and reveal a hidden paperfold. On December 2, cut the tape of the next card, etc.

You can use the same idea for making a "surprise" calendar for a sick person or for someone going on a trip. The person begins each day by opening a new window.

Decorating Halls: Decorating large spaces inexpensively often presents problems, but folded paper is ideal for auditoriums, gymnasiums and banquet rooms. Giant, multi-colored pinwheels, fans and stars are among the most effective decorations when attached to walls, suspended overhead or elevated from the floor by means of wooden dowels or rods secured in pots.

Greeting Cards and Wall Pictures

Most paperfolds suitable for greeting cards can also be used for posters when made in larger sizes. In a never-failing design scheme, glue three of a kind into triangular arrangements, all in the same or different colors.

Mobiles and Ornaments

Because paperfolds are light in weight they make excellent mobiles or hanging ornaments. Suspended from ceilings, near corners of rooms, in stairwells, and above a baby's crib, they turn gently in moving air currents.

Hanging Methods: Sewing thread or nylon filament (fishing line) are suitable for suspending the paperfolds. With a threaded needle pierce a hole at the top of the paperfold and knot on a length of thread. Attach the end of the thread to the ceiling with a piece of the kind of invisible cellophane tape that leaves no mark, or from the kind of ceiling hook used for hanging potted plants.

Balancing Point: Suspend symmetrical paperfolds, like the Surprising Triangle, from the center. With the Talking Whale and other figures that balance unevenly, you must find the balancing point. Make a hole with a needle where you think it might be and hold the needle in the air to let the paperfold balance from it. If the back of the paperfold is lower than the front, then make another hole with the needle in another position and try again. Do this until the paperfold balances properly. You can then knot a length of thread to that balancing hole.

You can also use the "two-string" method for balancing. Knot two pieces of thread to the top of the figure, slightly apart. Hold the threads together above the paperfold, letting it dangle in the air, and lengthen or shorten one of the threads until the object balances properly. Knot the threads together at this point. Cut off the remaining length of one piece of thread and use the other length for hanging.

Chain: You can suspend a flock of birds or several other paperfolds, one above the next.

Knot a thread to the top of the lowest unit and to the bottom of the next highest one, leaving about 1½ inches (4 cm) in between. Repeat this procedure between all units. Finally attach a good length of thread for hanging the mobile.

Home Accessories and Table Toppings

It is often possible to fill a bare spot in a room with paperfolds. They may be sprayed with acrylic (available in most art supply stores) for longer life and easier dusting.

Table Toppings: Paperfolds are ideal for centerpieces and party table decorations. For a summer theme, you can use boats surrounded by whales. You can frame the scene with a Christmas Wreath made from water-blue paper. Color coordinate them with paper Candy Dishes and Napkin Rings. For a festive touch, put shiny ornaments in all the empty spots on a table.

Folded Napkins: Complete a table setting with paper or fabric napkins folded into duck shapes or other simple designs.

Gifts

Craftspeople often search for new and different birthday and holiday gifts. Paper folding can, of course, fulfill this need uniquely. A handcrafted knick-knack makes a good gift for the person who has everything, as does a mobile for a baby, and a package of four or more greeting cards in a clear plastic bag for other friends.

Giftwraps: Attach a bird made from paper to the wrapping or let a paper snake meander over the top of a box. You can make a particularly dramatic presentation by taping a straw to the corner of the gift package and attaching a star or other design to the top of the straw. Glue several ducks in a row or a circle on the same package. Any of the ideas suggested for greeting cards or wall pictures can be used for decorating boxes.

Paperfolds that lie flat are especially suitable for trimming gift packages to be carried in suitcases or sent through the mail. Children usually enjoy receiving several paper bugs on the packages I send. You can make them easily detachable by using rubber cement instead of white glue.

Shower Memento: After a shower or other gift-giving occasion, collect all the gift-wrapping carefully. Cut it into squares. Fashion these into birds, frogs and mobiles, as a memento for the bride or baby.

Chinese Zodiac: Twelve symbolic animals are associated with the twelve- year cycle of the Chinese calendar: mouse (rat), ox, tiger, rabbit (hare), dragon, snake, horse, sheep, monkey, rooster (cock), dog, boar (pig). The sign of the year in which a person is born is said to influence personality and character. The symbolic meanings for the animal projects shown in this book are:

Rabbit:	Affectionate and lucky with money. 1987, 1999 (pg. 37)
Snake:	Enigmatic and intellectual. 1977, 1989 (pg. 72)
Rooster:	Conservative and witty. 1981, 1993 (pg. 58)
Dog:	Likeable and intelligent. 1982, 1994 (pg. 19)
Pig:	Honest and courageous. 1983, 1995 (pg. 62)
Mouse:	Hardworking and prosperous. 1984, 1996 (pg. 88)

You can use paperfolded animals for birthday cards, noting the significance of the animal. Or use them for decorations at Chinese New Year and other occasions.

Earning Money

Paperfolding is a wonderful hobby, but often when you give away a Jumping Frog or Finger Puppet someone will say, "Why don't you sell them?"

Most paperfolders, of course, are satisfied to share their creations freely, and yet there are some ways to make a little money with them. Greeting cards are the best sellers. They are in demand at museum shops, gift shops and stationery stores, which are always on the lookout for unusual merchandise. The cards must be packaged in plastic or cellophane envelopes. Plastic sandwich bags are probably the most convenient envelopes to use for this purpose. If you supply the paperfolds, you may wish to sign your name on the back of the cards.

The person who makes the paperfolds is expected to determine the retail price and to sell them to the store for one-third or one-half less than that price. If you decide the price of a card should be $2.00, for example, then the store will pay you $1.33 or $1.00 for each card. You usually receive the higher price if you leave your work on consignment, receiving payment only after the cards are sold.

Mobiles and cleverly-crafted party invitations are becoming popular with party givers. This is another possible source of income for you. An invitation may be three-dimensional and made up of many parts, like an old-fashioned valentine. Hosts and professional party organizers are always looking for novel ideas and will include the cost of invitations in their budgets.

You can also offer your services to a local bank for a seasonal promotion in return for a fee. You can arrange with the bank manager that you will sit in the bank lobby for a period of time and fold customers' dollar bills into bow ties. You can suggest placing a display case with folded dollar bills in the lobby prior to the event to attract customers.

Until recently an executive of the Chinese Imperial Court, Cai Lun, was credited with the invention of paper in A.D. 105. The date is known because the Chinese historian Fan Ye of the 6th century says that this man, who was an inspector in the Imperial workshops, invented and produced the first paper, presenting it to the Emperor in that year. The revolutionary achievement consisted in floating a fiber mixture of tree bark, hemp and linen in water, straining it through a sieve and letting it dry flat.

But Cai Lun's fame as the original papermaker has now been challenged. Remnants of hemp paper dated to 49 B.C. were discovered in China, in 1957, in Baqiao near Xian in Shaanxi Province. The paper included a small amount of ramie combined with the hemp. In 1973-74 specimens of hemp paper made during the Western Han Dynasty (206 B.C.-A.D. 24) were found at the old site of Jinguan of the Han Dynasty, and more was found from the same period in 1978 in Fufeng County of Shaanxi Province. These examples show that paper was invented by the Chinese more than 2,000 years ago.

The role of Cai Lun appears to be that of an improver of the coarse hemp paper of the Western Han Dynasty. He presented the emperor with a fine- quality paper which he produced by organizing the abundant man-power and natural resources of the court. The technique of papermaking spread to all parts of China from that time.

Before the widespread use of paper in China, written records were kept on tortoise shell, bone, metals, stones, bamboo slips, wooden tablets and silk. None of these materials, however, suited the need. Tortoise shell was scarce, metal and stone cumbersome, silk costly and bamboo slips and wooden tablets took up too much space.

Experimentation over the years resulted in the vegetable-fibre paper. The hemp that was used probably came from rope ends, rags and worn-out fishing nets.

Written records in other parts of the world were kept on silk, bone, stone, animal skins and other surfaces. Parchment was usually prepared from stretched sheep skins, but two other materials that were used are somewhat similar to paper: papyrus, which originated in Egypt, and tapa, produced in the Pacific basin and in Africa. Like paper these were made from vegetable fibers, but differ in the manufacturing process. The materials were beaten into flat sheets, and did not involve water flotation. That is what distinguishes true papermaking.

The technique of papermaking found its way through Korea to Japan in the 7th century and was introduced into Arabia through Central Asia in the middle of the 8th century. The first workshops at Baghdad in Iraq, Damascus in Syria and Samarkand in Central Asia were established with the assistance of Chinese craftsmen. The earliest hemp paper made from rags in Arabia was manufactured using methods and equipment quite similar to those used in China. After Arabian paper was being mass produced, it was exported to European countries in large quantities, and through Arabia the art of papermaking came to be introduced into Europe.

The first European countries to set up paper mills were Spain and France in the 12th century. By the 16th century, paper was extensively used in Europe and finally completely replaced the traditional parchment and Egyptian papyrus. From then on, papermaking continued on a westward

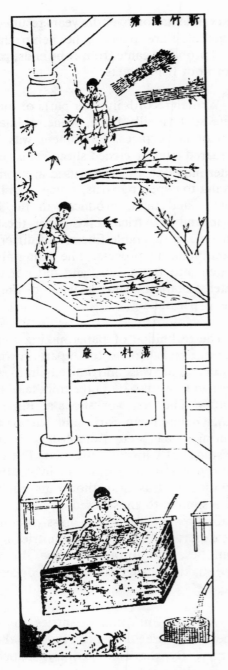

Papermaking in China as illustrated in Tiangong Kaiwu *published in 1637.*

course to Mexico and the United States, where the first mill was built in Pennsylvania in 1690.

The best quality papers include a high "rag" content. Street dealers used to collect worn-out cotton clothing, which factories converted into paper. Nowadays most commercial papers begin with shredded wood pulp, but superior papers still contain a percentage of fabric rags.

Paper was made by hand until the invention of machinery in the 18th century. Whether by hand or machine, all paper making methods are based on the principle of floating pulp in water. In hand papermaking, single sheets of paper are made one at a time. Machine-made paper is produced in huge rolls. The process begins with pulp being distributed evenly onto screens on block-long machines. Conveyor belts keep rolling the material along, while it is squeezed into the required thickness, dried, rolled up and finally cut into the desired sheet size. Commercial papers are produced in an immense variety of brilliant colors, thicknesses and quality for all kinds of purposes.

With the ease of producing large quantities by mechanical means, making paper by hand became increasingly rare until the 1970's. Then artists began to appreciate the individuality of a handmade sheet. Hand papermaking has since been revived as a craft. Such handmade sheets are used for printing limited editions of graphics, portfolios and books. Paper of this type also sometimes becomes the medium itself, with the color and texture of the material being shaped into works of art.

HISTORY OF PAPERFOLDING

Whether it is called "zhe zhi," as it is by Mandarin-speaking Chinese, or "chip chee," as Chinese who use the Cantonese dialect call it, or by the Japanese name "origami," it is generally agreed that the art of paperfolding originated in China perhaps before the 6th century.

Reverence for ancestors was a guiding principle of Chinese life in ancient times, and the living tried to maintain a close link to the dead. As early as the Shang and Zhou dynasties (1500-256 B.C.) elaborate ceremonies for funerals and annual festivals were observed to honor the dead. The deceased were presumed to have the same needs as the living, and tombs were stocked with ceramic replicas of everyday furnishings to provide all possible comforts in the afterworld.

Ceramics were later replaced with paper, but additional research is needed to reveal when this change took place. Paper replicas of worldly goods included clothing, farm animals, treasure chests, and any other desirable object. Often these were made of colorful paper that was cut, folded and pasted over bamboo strips. Some funeral items, such as gold nuggets, were folded only, without any cutting and gluing. Intead of being buried in tombs, the paper artifacts were burned, accompanied by prayers in prescribed rituals.

Though such religious practices have been officially discouraged in the People's Republic of China since Liberation in 1949, they do continue to some extent in country villages. They flourish in many Chinese communities outside of China. In Hong Kong and Singapore paper houses, luxury cars, refrigerators and chests filled with gold nuggets are common at some Chinese funerals. In the West very little is known about these customs, and I believe my collection of funerary paper artifacts is unique.

Paperfolding, like most folk crafts, is usually transmitted from one generation to another. To this day grandmothers in China teach and entertain their grandchildren with paper toys. Paperfolding is also taught in kindergarten to improve students' manual dexterity.

The fact that paper crafts are popular at all levels of the Chinese population was strikingly domonstrated during the first days of April in 1976, when millions of Chinese spontaneously gathered at the Monument of Heroes in Beijing's Tian An Men Square to commemorate the life of Premier Zhou Enlai, who had died three months earlier. Mountains of paper flowers were piled high around the monument, and this is believed to be the largest use of paper decorations at any one time. At least half of these paper flowers were made by young and old men. The occasion, later known as the "Tiananmen Incident," precipitated the downfall of the "Gang of Four" and signalled a new stage in China's history.

The best known Chinese paperfolds are the Chinese Balloon, Candy Dish, Chinese Pagoda Tower and Chinese Junk. Small folded packets for carrying incense and other things, indicating the usual Chinese preference for folding objects rather than animals or plants, are also popular paperfolds in China. In some stores paperfolding is an everyday occurrence, as groceries and medicines are wrapped in paper cones rather than being placed in manufactured bags. The shop assistant takes a paper square, rolls it into a cone, fills it with rice, flour, beans or other food or medicine, flops over the top corner and tucks this in to secure the contents. In dispensaries, small quantities of herbal medicines are usually placed in the center of a piece of paper that is then folded into a flat packet.

Finally, Chinese boys often play a game with pieces of paper folded into triangles. A player throws his triangle on the ground attempting to strike that of another player. The opponent's triangle becomes a forfeit if it turns over when it is hit. I have no information about the folding method.

Japan

Paperfolding, or origami, has been most highly developed in Japan. It is believed that the art was imported to Japan and Korea from China in the seventh century, at the same time as the process of making paper was introduced from China to those countries.

The earliest Japanese reference to paperfolding occurs in a manuscript of the Edo Period (1614-1868). Here it mentions a box of pre-folded origami figures, implying that such collections were available for sale as long ago as 1728. (See a privately circulated essay: "Paper Folding in Japan," by David Lister, an English paperfolder.) "Kanomado," a book dating to the mid-nineteenth century, is considered the oldest comprehensive treatise on paperfolding. (See "A Japanese Paperfolding Classic" by Julia and Martin Brossman, The Pinecone Press, Washington, D.C., 1961.) The "Kanomodo" contains instructions for making a dragonfly, butterflies, a wrestler going into the ring, a monkey, traditional dolls and many other objects. This list indicates the Japanese preference for folding life forms rather than inanimate objects.

Paper folded in prescribed forms, called "Noshi," were traditionally used as wrappers for gifts, and symbolized good wishes. At the present time, in Japan, such stylized designs in simplified forms are still attached to gifts—like small gift cards—but are of interest to Westerners mostly as forerunners of contemporary paperfolding.

Children learn origami at home and in elementary schools. As a result most Japanese adults can remember how to fold a crane and one or two other things. The crane is a traditional symbol of good fortune and longevity, and it has now also become a symbol of peace. According to a Japanese legend, anyone who folds 1,000 cranes will be granted a wish. This tradition inspired Sadako Sasaki, a little girl who survived the bombing of Hiroshima, to attempt this task. Unfortunately she was not able to complete it before she died of leukemia. Her story inspired the building of a Peace Memorial in Hiroshima.

Every year children from many parts of Japan and many other countries send thousands and thousands of folded paper cranes to an annual ceremony held in Hiroshima to promote peace. Ploughshares, a group based in Seattle, Washington, now sponsors the "Million Cranes Project". Schools and other groups commit themselves to sending 1,000 cranes to world leaders in the cause of peace. One crane from each 1,000 contributions is sent to the gravesite of Sadako Sasaki.

Origami has developed into an elaborate adult art form, with exhibitions being held in Japan from time to time for the best examples of this art. Akira Yoshisawa is considered the most prominent origami artist. Since 1966, Yoshisawa has traveled to over thirty countries in order to spread the art of origami. And in 1983 he was decorated by the Emperor of Japan for his efforts to promote friendly relations among nations of the world with this craft. Before portraying any particular animal with folded paper, Yoshisawa studies its anatomy and habits for long periods of time so as to be able to imbue his creation with the animal's characteristics and soul. His original paperfolds are quite spectacular.

United States and Other Western Countries

The airplane and the paper hat that turns into a boat are the paperfolds that are best known in the United States and Europe.

Leonardo da Vinci is considered the earliest European experimenter with paperfolding. Other famous folders include Samuel Johnson, Lewis Carroll, Unamuno, Houdini, and the convicted banker Michael Sidona. During the 18th and 19th centuries it was customary in Germany to fold baptisimal certificates and other religious documents in decorative ways. The beginning steps shown for making the Fortune Teller were a common configuration used for such certificates. In 1837 the German educator, Friedrich Froebel, originated kindergarten schooling in Germany and included paperfolding in his curriculum.

Paperfolding gained impetus in the United States in the late 1950's as a result of the work of Lillian Oppenheimer, the founder of the Origami Center in New York, and in England as a result of the work of Robert Harbin, a magician who presented a series of paperfolding programs on television in

London. In 1959 the Cooper Union Museum (now the Cooper-Hewitt Museum of the Smithsonian Institution) presented an exhibit of paperfolds in New York. It was entitled "Paper Geometry and Fancy Figures."

Paperfolders are always busiest at Christmas time, because paper ornaments are charming and easy to make. Every December a 60-foot tree decorated with thousands of animals is a regular feature at the American Museum of Natural History in New York City. And each Christmas other trees of this type appear at other locations. The White House Christmas tree in Washington, D.C., also occasionally has some folded ornaments.

In the United States, England, Spain, Italy, France and other Western countries, the craft has attracted many followers who have formed groups with regular meetings and newsletters. Through their activities, libraries, museums and other institutions have become aware of paperfolding as an art. Many offer exhibitions and workshops from time to time. More and more schools also recognize paperfolding as a useful and versatile educational tool, with a definite role in art and mathematics classes and for enrichment. Paperfolding has been particularly successful in occupational and psychiatric therapy.

Some skilled enthusiasts create highly sophisticated pieces. Such work may be shown in exhibitions dedicated specifically to paperfolding and mixed-media exhibitions held in museums and art galleries. Some forms may have only a few creases while others may have as many as 250. Artists who make paper by hand, are beginning to apply paperfolding techniques to achieve new sculptural forms.

HOW TO TEACH PAPERFOLDING

It's an exhilerating experience to teach paperfolding, because audiences respond enthusiastically. As you become proficient at this art, you may be asked to present programs at schools, in libraries, before art associations, and to many other groups. Or you may already be a teacher or scout leader with a class eager to learn the art. Whatever the case may be, here are some pointers you may find useful.

Preparation: Arrange to have all the participants seated at tables, if possible. Find out ahead of time the approximate number of people who will attend so that you can bring a sufficient supply of paper. The program organizer may offer to supply the paper, but I prefer to bring my own so as to be sure it is suitable.

Decide beforehand what projects you wish to teach, and go over all the steps in your mind repeatedly to set them firmly. With large groups I usually teach three or four fairly simple projects, such as the Chinese Duck, Gift Box, Party Hat, Icicle and Jumping Frog. I usually do not have such a set program for smaller groups, which I treat as informal workshops.

Assemble more than a sufficient amount of paper for each project you plan to teach. Most require squares, but some, such as the Gift Box, are made from rectangles. For myself, I use larger pieces of paper than the ones I distribute to the audience so that they can see clearly what I am doing.

The Program: Teach each pattern step by step. After each pattern is completed, I give the audience a rest by telling them some background information (much of which you can find in this book) and some amusing incidents I have experienced when folding.

The programs usually last about one hour. I always demonstrate the bird with flapping wings and people inevitably clamor to learn it. Because I can make it quite quickly, they usually think it can be learned in a couple of minutes. But it is more complex than it appears and I find it best not to teach it to a large group.

Schools: Paperfolding has many educational aspects and obviously aids eye-hand coordination by promoting small motor facilities. It has been found to be enriching for both learning-disabled and gifted students.

In schools, I gear the projects to the grade level and, if asked to do so, to a specific area of the curriculum. Paperfolding fits particularly well into social studies, art and math classes.

Students in social studies classes enjoy craft activities. You can reinforce your lessons on China or Japan by including some paperfolding. This craft in those countries is transmitted from one generation to another. Paperfolding thus brings home the importance of family life in the Orient and helps to increase the students' understanding of these cultures.

In art classes paperfolding offers students a three-dimensional art experience. A report entitled "Beyond Creating: The Place for Art in American Schools," published by the J. Paul Getty Trust, states that methods of teaching art are undergoing a rapid change and it recommends a broadening visual arts program that includes art production, art history, art criticism and aesthetics. In this context, paperfolding can help children become "better prepared to live in an increasingly technological world" by "understanding the meaning and beauty transmitted by the arts."

Paper can be used to demonstrate some mathematical facts much more graphically than drawings can. For example, to bisect an angle just fold the corner of a piece of paper in half. Or, unfold a Chinese Duck or other paperfold to let the students observe the various geometric forms shown by the creases in the paper.

Paperfolded puppets in language classes encourage verbal expression and story telling, and have produced remarkable results with the hearing-impaired.

Some teachers set aside an area stocked with paper and a book of paperfolding instructions for students who have completed their assignments. *Paper Pandas and Jumping Frogs* is suitable for students of all ages as it contains projects for beginners that lead up to a few more complicated projects.

Here are many types of paper you will find useful for all paperfolding projects.

Origami Paper: Best suited for most things in this book. Origami paper is already cut into squares, varying in size from 3'' (7 cm) to 10'' (25 cm). It usually comes packaged in one size only or in a combination of two or three sizes. Most paperfolders find the 6'' size most satisfactory, except for special projects. Each pack contains an assortment of bright colors. Paper with overall patterns is also available. Origami paper is sold in art supply stores, oriental stores and some gift shops.

The following papers must be cut into squares, with scissors, craft and utility knives along a straight edge or, most conveniently, a paper cutter.

Bond Paper: Typing and printing papers are least expensive and available in many colors. An 8½'' by 11'' sheet can be cut into two 5'' squares or one larger square. This type of paper is recommended for classroom use or whenever large quantities are required.

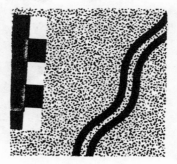

Computer Paper: Here is another source of inexpensive paper. Cut discarded printouts of a non-confidential nature into squares and use them in the classroom or for practising paperfolding.

Gift Wrap Paper: Exciting colors and graphics can make a world of difference to a paperfolded design, but cutting rolled paper into squares can be tedious. Paper with small overall patterns is usually best.

Construction Paper: This may be used for simple designs and large decorations.

Art Paper: This general term is applied to colored paper sold in art and school supply stores and through catalogs. It comes in many colors, is heavier than origami paper, and is therefore suitable for larger things.

Handmade Papers: The texture of handmade papers can enhance the hand-crafted quality of many paperfolds. It usually takes a little longer to fold with these papers, and very soft papers should be avoided. Try them also as background papers for greeting cards. Handmade Japanese sheets are sold in art supply and some museum stores.

Pages from Magazines: The weight of many magazine papers is excellent for paperfolding, and the bright colors from illustrations can provide unusual designs. Use the front and back covers of magazines for making paper boxes.

These are some of the best choices for paperfolding, but most hard-surfaced papers provide good creasing quality. I look at any piece of paper I come across to see whether it can be folded well. Try examining all sorts of everyday stationery and wrapping materials for possibilities as squares to be used in paperfolding. The inside of some bank envelopes suggests the texture of fur, and other pieces of paper just seem to want to be folded into a duck, box, or something else.

ACKNOWLEDGMENTS

Most black and white photographs by Richard Petersen. Others by Florence Temko and Ronald Temko.

Color photographs by David Friend.

Cover design by Kathleen McKeown.
Front cover photograph by Bernard Slabeck.

Paul Jackson, illustrator, is Editor of *British Origami*, an international monthly magazine published in England for paperfolding enthusiasts all over the world.

It is impossible to acknowledge the many sources which have inspired me over the years to write *Paper Pandas and Jumping Frogs*. I am deeply aware that this book is the result of age-old traditions of paperfolding and the contacts I have enjoyed for many years. Lillian Oppenheimer, founder and director of the Origami Center of New York has been my personal and paperfolding friend since before she began organizing origami enthusiasts all over the world. Alice Grey, Michael Shall and others of the Friends of the Origami Center; Paul Jackson and others of the British Origami Society; Akira Yoshisawa, President of the International Origami Centre; Toshie Takahama of the Nippon Origami Society; Dorothy Kaplan, Emanuel Mooser, Gwyneth Radcliffe, Joyce Rockmore, Francis Ow, and Lin Hee Sen all form part of my valued paperfolding circle. Others who have shown an interest in this project include Lydia Anyon of the U.S.-China Friendship Association and Cui Wei-jie of the Tianjin Municipal Library. Jane Bender, Mary Jane Bender, Lorraine Lauzon, Safija Sarich, and Mrs. Frye's third grade have helped in testing the instructions to make sure they can be followed step-by-step.

Authors usually mention their own families for their support, but this is no empty phrase. I thank Henry, most of all, and Joan, Bob, Ronald, Linda, Stephen, Ellen, Yolanda, Tyler, Janet, Loren and Dennis.

To my best knowledge the projects are either traditional or my designs. Yolanda Anyon at age 6 created the Monster Puppet, although a similar toy had been published by Lewis and Oppenheimer. The Rooster is a simplification of a design by Sam Randlett. The Panda is adapted from contemporary Japanese designs.

Paper Pandas and Jumping Frogs is my second book to be published by China Books & Periodicals, Inc., following *Chinese Papercuts*, and I particularly want to thank those in this publishing firm with whom I have worked most closely.

INDEX

ABOUT THE AUTHOR

Florence Temko is an internationally known artist and author of 21 books on paper arts and folk crafts. She has presented hundreds of hands-on programs in educational and industrial settings, including the Metropolitan Museum of Art in New York, the Children's Museum in Boston, the Mingei International Museum of Folk Craft in La Jolla, California, The Advertising Club, the Art Teachers' Association, The American Craft Fair, and the Technical Association of the Paper and Pulp Industry among many others.

She has appeared on many television programs including her own series of popular craft shows, and she has made three motion picture films of her work.

Florence Temko loves to fold paper and to share her enthusiasm in person and through her books. People often report that as soon as she meets you she is likely to make and present you with a paper bird that flaps its wings. She believes paper is a wonderful educational tool, but she also sees many uses for paper as home decoration and unusual party entertainments. She reportedly knows how to fold paper squares into 1,800 different things, and is constantly looking for more variations.

Florence Temko has traveled in 31 countries in search of paper folk craft traditions. She is listed in "Who's Who of American Women." She was educated in England and, after living in Lenox, Massachusetts, now makes her home in San Diego, California.